Praise for

ATOMOS

"Inspired by Mallette's deep research into political philosophy, myth, and dystopian literature from Shelley to Atwood, *Atomos* is a tour de force debut in the cutting-edge subgenre of sci-fi known as cli-fi. A compelling read for all ages."

—Eileen M. Hunt
Author of *Artificial Life After Frankenstein*

ATOMOS

CLW MALLETTE

Atomos

by CLW Mallette

ISBN 978-1-64663-610-5

Published by

Mallette Books

"You can't talk about nuclear power until you've explained the fact that atoms have nuclei. You can't talk about the conversion of matter into energy without talking about relativity and quantum mechanics."
—Neal Stephenson (2008)

"The story without God is about atoms."
—Margaret Atwood (2006)

"It was sea and islands now; the great continent had sunk like Atlantis."
—C. S. Lewis (1955)

"By attributing electricity to the constitution of the atom, it causes the atoms to become purveyors of death. Physicists continue to put forward [this attribution as] an atomic theory and decide everywhere to matter. As soon as the atomic form is identified with electricity, it also identifies nature with evil. In that case, atoms composed of electrons are tiny evil demons."
—Rudolf Steiner (1923)

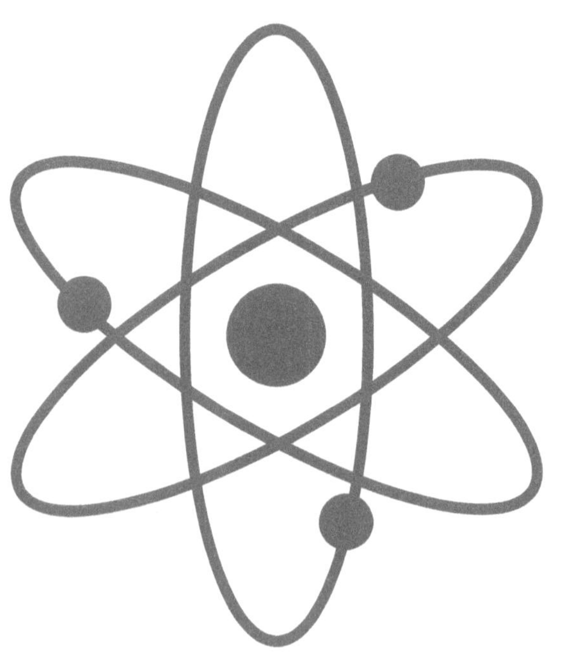

TABLE OF CONTENTS

Time was against the people of Easter Island. With no foreign contact in centuries, the dreams of their eldest prophets shifted toward preservation. According to ancient wisdom, warriors were chosen to compete in a race to reach an eagle's nest, proving their worth to the tribe. After swimming through shark-infested waters to reach the egg, they'd need to return to the main island unharmed. Only then could a warrior be made Birdman. Immortalized in stone, their statues are largely considered the last remnants of their culture. Nothing was left but their heads, facing outward.

Still, so much remained hidden in the waters around Easter Island, drowned in mystery. Other than their legend of Atlantis, what could possibly have prepared explorers for the truth? Blind to those possibilities, they hastily left Easter Island, far more confused than when they'd arrived. Although their search led to nowhere, in each and every case, a calm always comes before the storm.

Science fiction and nonfiction have each taken direction from Captain

Cook's infamous exploration of the South Pacific, filled with tales of places "farther than any man has been before." Although his perilous search for a new world has long guided history's hand, her other hand might uncover a different story. Bordered by Easter Island, Hawaii, and New Zealand, the Polynesian Triangle isn't a new world. The explorers were just new. Even along the outermost stretch of Oceania, in and among the oddest bits of the world's forgotten frontier, humans are still always the same, for better or worse. Our first and greatest taboo is complete extinction, not simple exploration. Once again, we humans are guided by the wisdom of dreams and prophecies: one day, there will be a child, born equally from the elements of light and darkness, destined to oversee the long-foretold battle between man and nature.

THE BOY WHO WAS LOST

Footprints in the sand would forever remind him of the stars and the moon. The soft echo that sang in her voice followed him for years, like his lonely shadow. "Did you see all the lovely silver blues?" it whispered.

Harsh, sandy wind blew up against the feathers of a perched albatross, tearing away the flesh of a round blue fish in its claws. The bird sat atop a red, wooden fence broken at the ends rather than sawn through. Five sandy surfboards leaned against it, all of different sorts and sizes, and some far more badly worn than others. Sharp knicks and long scratches adorned each of the boards' faces. Atomos grabbed the shortest one, not only because he was himself very short but because it was the fastest and could cut through waves with the most ease.

He ran out onto the beach with unhinged enthusiasm, surfboard under his arm. Red hair flowed in the wind, exposing his round, freckled ears. Atomos was covered in freckles, head to toe, and wore a dark-green swimsuit with cargo pockets. His eyes were a dim gray, like metal or ash. Behind Atomos, his caretaker, Pueo, walked slowly. Perhaps it was the limp, but Pueo had more of a cautious air about him. He was a large man, taller than six feet, and very round in the belly. He wore no shirt and had no tattoos, but his skin was dark and his eyes brown. Pueo's hair and beard were long, black, and ridden with thick tangles; however, much of it was gray, soon to be speckled white. He slipped off his pink flip-flops in the sand and walked patiently after the boy, surfboard also in hand. His swimsuit was black, matching the shark-tooth necklace that rested around his shoulders. The waves crashed in the water ahead of them, peaks white and foamy. Four or five fluffy clouds dotted a wide-open, azure sky.

As Atomos pointed the tip of his surfboard directly into the ocean and perpendicular from the horizon, a tall wave rose from the depths and towered over him, just inches above his head. *Splash!* The tide rushed over him in a frenzy. Then, just as quickly, it disappeared. Dripping down his curly red hair and onto the tan board between his hands, the pool of water glistened in the sun. Immediately, Atomos felt at home.

Sand stuck to his swim shorts. The grains in between his fingers and toes washed away. Ahead, to his left and right, blue waves rose nearly ten or fifteen feet over his head. Nothing bigger came around these parts until hurricane season. Atomos turned, facing the nose of his board back toward the beach. Two faded blue stripes were painted longwise on each side of his board, perfectly parallel to one another. Lying facedown on them, he brought his hands up from paddling and placed them firmly beside his chest, palms flat. In one quick motion, he pushed his body and tucked his feet under himself, like he'd done a thousand times before. Then, ever so slightly, he moved his right foot forward to center his balance.

Atomos let his arms out to each side, loose and extended. Feet planted firmly, he bent his knees and hunkered down even lower. His torso leaned forward, further lowering his center of gravity. As Atomos stuck his hand behind him and into the water, a plethora of bubbles burst from beneath his fingertips. Before long, they stretched over three times his height. Gliding along the surface of the water, Atomos felt an extreme rush of air and ocean spray. There was something so natural about the way it moved him.

Sitting down on his board in calmer waters, he noticed a magnificent sea turtle swimming directly under his feet. The dark creature had a long, streamlined pattern upon its shell. It almost looked like a plastic bag. The view was slightly distorted by the shifting water, but as Atomos focused, he could see well enough. She appeared something of a lovely olive green, with perhaps a hint of brown. Although Pueo had always said not to touch them, he was so far away. There was no way he'd see below the water. Atomos dove his whole arm in. The creature's limbs flapped furiously, and it darted away before Atomos could get close. Even turtles were too fast for him.

"Atomos?" shouted Pueo from across the waves. He paddled over to the boy and then sat up on his board, next to Atomos. "I've told you a thousand times. Don't touch the turtles, Atomos, not even if they swim right up next to you. It's illegal. They're endangered. We don't want them to think humans are safe."

The boy was distracted. He didn't care what Pueo had to say about Hawaiian law. How could he? Pueo stood up for the law one moment and criticized it the next.

"For being close to a hundred years old, she moved well in the water. I wonder if she wanted to get back to her family? Oh, I'm sorry, Pueo. I didn't mean to mention—"

Pueo knew what Atomos was trying to do, but he also understood that being free-spirited and restless was only natural at his age, especially for Atomos, who'd been stuck on an island his entire life. Pueo thought it better to entertain and educate than to ridicule; this, at least, was more rewarding. Most of all, Pueo wanted Atomos to be happy.

"It's okay, Atomos. I'm glad to be here. Today's the anniversary of the day we met, you know, her and I?" Pueo lost himself in a memory. "Even though I know you can't remember, she thought the world of you, Atomos. She thought of you like a son." Atomos said nothing. "Well, anyway, of course they're fast," added Pueo naturally. He had no problem changing the topic himself. "Turtles outlived the dinosaurs, for heaven's sake. Why do you think that is?"

"Like, it was so much longer in the grand scheme of things. How many years did dinosaurs eat turtles before they went extinct?" replied Atomos coldly, staring off toward the island.

"Well, if we don't slow down now, they'll all go extinct, won't they?"

"Never mind," sighed Atomos.

The sun was low in the sky, touching the edge of the water. Pueo felt the warmth on his back. He smiled despite the pain in his heart. Forming his hand into a cup and lowering it into the water beside his surfboard, Pueo lifted a handful of seawater to his face and let it fall out from between his fingers, splashing onto his board. "Water!" he exclaimed. "They hid under the water!"

"The day's almost over, Pueo. I want to get back before it gets too dark. Hopefully, I can finish my book." Atomos leaned forward onto his chest and began paddling away before Pueo had the chance to respond. He glided over the miniature waves with ease. As the boy paddled back to the island by his lonesome, distracted, Pueo couldn't help but feel as though this might be one of the last times he'd go surfing with his adopted son.

Atomos walked inland, dragging his feet in the sand. He felt a strange prick on his heel. That was different. A fishing hook had wedged into his thick skin. *How'd that happen?* he wondered, pinching it between his fingers and tearing its grip away from his flesh. He hadn't worn shoes in two years, at least, not since his red pair lost their soles. Tearing new ones apart could only add so much character. Nonchalantly, Atomos tossed his surfboard against the others leaning on the red, weatherworn fence. As it collided with them, the seabird perched on the far post squawked and flew away into the jungle. Hopefully, that was the last of them.

He mounted the green hill in his bare feet. Not a drop of blood escaped his body. The grass brushed away the sand stuck to his ankles and his calves, but never as well as in the water. All at once, starting in his shoulders and spreading throughout his entire body, a feeling of calmness rushed over Atomos like a tidal wave. He was alone now—finally, alone.

The hut in which Atomos lived was made from richly colored koa wood. In Hawai'i, in addition to being a building material, the word *koa* also meant a brave, fearless warrior; Atomos liked this comparison. Nothing scared him. Still, not everything in the hut was so grand and symbolic. The windows were small and crooked. The steps up to the base of the hut were also wooden, and the door was made of hanging palm leaves. The roof hung over each side by over a foot, constructed by binding the leaves of palm trees together and tying them to the hard, dark wooden posts. Atomos liked to say the hut was both of theirs, but he hadn't built it; Pueo had. Still, with the bed he had on his boat, Pueo hadn't slept there in years. "Why sleep on an island?" That's what he always said.

The highest ridge on the island cast its large shadow over their hut. Standing in front of the shelter, Atomos focused on a tall, thin palm tree growing out from underneath its flooring. As Atomos stared up at its dark trunk, he couldn't help but remember the moment when, four or five years earlier, at the age of ten, he'd climbed the tree during a storm. He'd never been very down to earth. When Atomos climbed something, he climbed it all the way to the top. Reaching for the sun that poked out from the clouds in the storm, Atomos was struck by a bolt of lightning and fell violently to the ground. Ever since then, Atomos had been more thoughtful, prone to meditate rather than to tempt fate. Even this change, however, would elevate his ambitions. Often, when the winds howled, Atomos watched the trees shake, unimpressed. He chuckled. Who made this little monsoon? Was it some Lord of the Skies, someone for the winds to call master, or was this just a gust?

Directly across from the door, inside the right-hand corner of the hut, was a paint-chipped, white gas stove with two small, rusted burners and only a single black metal knob. Where the other should be, there was only an empty hole. Despite being pushed back against an adjacent wall, his single bed filled the room. To the right of the bed, a silver-and-black telescope pointed out the window, looking up at the stars. How strange was it that Neil A. walked on the moon? Now and forever, he has written his name into history, but if he had written it backward, he'd have spelled Alien. How strange. The black logo on the side of the telescope read *Ou muamua*,[1] one of Atomos's all-time favorite Hawaiian phrases. Although Atomos had moved beyond studying the solar system, he still quite enjoyed the occasional night of looking at the stars. Of all the planets, he most admired the dwarves[2] orbiting beyond the Kuiper belt.

A large bookshelf stood to the side, full to the brim with books, a few even spilling out at the bottom. Atomos counted four books scattered alongside the bed: two of them lay facedown, directly on their pages, one was faceup and open, and only one, the last one, was properly closed as a book ought to be. On the floorboards under the books lay a beautiful and ornate circular rug with a zigzag pattern along its circumference. Red and yellow, its design was obviously intended to represent the sun, although Atomos doubted the sun ever had a fixed shape. Despite its wear and tear, not a single stitch was out of place. Above, a circular fan spun in an off-center, gyrating fashion. Its blue-and-white seashells doubled as a light fixture; still, they were very dim. Their texture was interesting, though—very rough, almost spiky. There was no refrigerator and no clock.

Atomos took one of the books off the floor, a paperback copy of *Frankenstein*. He walked to the edge of the island where a long, droopy palm tree hung off the cliff. Atomos got as close to the edge as he could and jumped, fearlessly. He grabbed hold of the trunk in midair and pulled himself up. Heights didn't scare Atomos even a little. Pueo used to joke that he was part monkey. However, when Atomos turned back, he saw

---

1   In 2017, a telescope in Hawaiʻi discovered the first known interstellar object to pass through our solar system. In Hawaiian, the name means "reach out for" (ou) and "first, in advance of" (muamua). Usually, this would refer to an unexpected visitor from a far-off land.

2   Pluto: the Greek god of the underworld and the most infamous of the dwarves, the dwarf planet Pluto partially orbits its moon, Charon.
Eris: the Roman god of chaos, this entirely white planet has slightly more mass than Pluto but also is just a little smaller. Its moon's name is Dysnomia, a mental condition most associated with the difficulty of remembering names.
Haumea: a Hawaiian goddess whose moons/daughters are Hiʻiaka and Namaka. Most notable for its elongated egg shape, the planet has four-hour days, a red spot, and a ring.
Makemake: the third largest of the dwarf planets, this brown-and-red rock is named after the chief deity of Easter Island.
Qua-oar: a Native American god/planet, whose moon is called Weywot.
Gonggong: a Chinese deity with an iron forehead and red hair.
The Goblin: this one had a thirty-thousand-year orbit.
Last, there was Orcus and Selacia.

the flowers he'd accidentally stepped on: birds of paradise, broken at the stem. At first, Atomos felt remorse, but then he felt the winds of change blow around him. Atomos gazed up into the sky. Having set, the sun had left brilliant shades of orange and pink in its place. Already, the stars and the moon were shining bright. The universe was so big. What use was it to get upset over something so small? Leaves came and went with the seasons. Death was unavoidable. As Atomos read, he forgot all about the flowers, whose beauty he'd already determined was fleeting. He stayed up long into the night, reading under the moonlight. The ever-present waves carried on, crashing on the rocks below, rocking him into a sound, soothing sleep.

A WALK ON THE BEACH

2

The fire pit was smoldering and red hot under a pile of lava rocks that had been collected over the years. Atomos remembered them all fondly. At low tide, the best time for collecting, he'd take walks around the island's perimeter. It also gave him a chance to be alone, something Atomos had wanted for a while.

Atomos was jolted back into reality as the smell of smoke filled his senses. He stepped away from the fire and walked across the unkempt yard that lay outside his and Pueo's hut, past two chairs, over to a tall, green banana tree. Using nothing but his bare hands, Atomos tore down several leaves to cover the pit with. *Snap! Snap!* The leaves were nearly six feet tall, each easily taller than him by a whole foot. They were dark green everywhere except their spines. Atomos walked back with the banana leaves hoisted over his shoulder. A thin cloud of smoke rose from the fire. Atomos hoped Pueo would be back before it was completely burned. But then, just as quickly as the thought occurred to him, Atomos remembered he didn't care. He dropped the banana leaves beside the pit, walked around the fire, past the hut, down the grassy slope, and beyond his hammock. It was time for a walk.

The sun beat down heavily as Atomos walked through the sand, leaving footprint after footprint in his wake. A few more hours would pass before it took its full position in the sky. A long shadow stretched out in front of him as Atomos walked, kicking sand. Still, his shadow was small compared to the spots of shade uphill, resting under the palm trees. Atomos felt ambivalent toward them, or, at least, that's what he told himself. He was on a mission.

Trash was everywhere. Atomos picked up bottle after bottle. Blue plastic pens and see-through ear picks were buried deep within the wet sand. He could be out here all day and nothing would change. There was no end in sight. Sure, he could get the big pieces, but that wouldn't do much, not everything considered. The smaller the segment, he remembered, the more dangerous. All life in the sea was threatened, from the octopuses to the whales. Nobody held out, not even the walrus. Atomos hated to imagine this future.

Turning the corner to the far side of the island, Atomos suddenly caught a glimpse of what had to be the most vile and disturbing sight he'd ever seen: a beached whale festering in the heat. The sight of blood and blubber was gut-wrenching. Flocking to the carcass, seabirds squawked, fighting over scraps. Bits of exposed bone stuck out close to the whale's stomach. Atomos rushed over, kicking through sand and trash, swatting his hands back and forth. Death was no joke; it was more real than anything. Looking down at the creature's lifeless form, Atomos was bothered most of all by how the creature died. Unable to breathe or roll back into the ocean, it had suffered, slowly. If that wasn't agony, what was? Would nature be as cruel to him? Perhaps it was time itself that was cruel. Did it ever feel regret? There was no way of knowing, not for sure. The only question remaining, Atomos realized, was what to do now.

Atomos lifted the tail of the colossus, hoisting it over his shoulders. A full-grown blue whale would be more difficult to carry than banana leaves. Still, Pueo was getting old. Atomos didn't want him to walk too far. Plus, his dock would make for a good place to gut and clean the whale. He gripped the tail tight, squeezing it between his forearm and bicep. Atomos raised the slippery fin over his right shoulder. He reached across his chest with his left arm, securing the beast. As Atomos pulled, his mind began to wander.

In the old days, Pueo used to tell him how, when he was much smaller, his name wasn't Atomos, it was Little One. That was it, just Little One. What a name. What did it matter? Although Atomos didn't have much recollection of those days, Pueo had told him the story of how he'd found his actual name more than once.

Pueo would recall how he knew, instantly, that the young child had special powers. However, it took him about five or six more years to name him Atomos. Stronger and more thick-skinned than any baby Pueo had ever seen, the boy needed a powerful name to match his powerful ability. Pueo didn't want to give Atomos a Hawaiian name like his own. The boy clearly wasn't Hawaiian. Red hair and freckles weren't common anywhere in the South Pacific, even to this day. Instead, Pueo believed he could find a better name for the boy in the history books.

Although he considered the names of two of the greatest demigod warriors, Hercules and Achilles, Pueo was deterred by the tragic way each of their lives ended. Should he want the rituals of the ancient world to shape the child's destiny? He certainly hadn't been given a choice. Still, Pueo deeply admired the ancient Greeks for their philosophy, even though none could see the color blue—at least, according to the Odyssey, which included every other color. Pueo was determined to find a name to bridge this gap and reconnect the past to the future. Then, one day, Pueo found the name he'd been searching for in a book on science and philosophy: Atomos.

It was perfect. For years, Pueo told Atomos he'd chosen the name because it meant the boy could write his own destiny, but that was only a portion of the truth. Atomos was named after a scientific term used by the ancient Greeks. To them, science and philosophy were very much one and the same. The philosopher who coined the term, Democritus, often used the word *Atomos* to describe the smallest, most uncuttable thing he could imagine. To Pueo, the matter of naming the child Atomos seemed so natural, it was beyond his control; it was destiny. *However, now,* Atomos thought, *humans know the structure of an atom is more complex.* There were so many smaller pieces. An atom was filled with protons, neutrons, and even an electron cloud, not to mention quarks. They were even smaller, held together by gluons. So, in the end, atoms weren't the smallest units in the universe, and as everyone in the South Pacific now remembered, neither were they indestructible.

Atomos trudged along, dragging the whale carcass through the center of the jungle. With each step up the hill, he felt the creature's weight tugging back at him. The muscles on his neck and shoulder strained under its weight. Atomos paused to take a break. Before long, however, he was back at it. Suddenly, a large, bubbly waterfall stood in his path. He'd heard it before seeing it. This, too, he would try and surmount, even with the whale on his back. Atomos loved a challenge.

After nearly two hours of hard work, Atomos arrived at the base of the dock, peering out at Pueo's boat where the fisherman spent the majority of his time. It was a small boat, size enough for only a single person to comfortably live. A single bed and a stove were on board, along with half a dozen pots and pans. There was a radio, too. The radio equipment stuck out of the roof a whole six feet, maybe more. From the top, Pueo flew a Hawaiian flag upside down. He always had. Out in the open ocean, the old fisherman had seen it all.

"Pueo!" yelled Atomos. "Come out here! Look! I've found something!"

"Wow! Atomos," replied Pueo, "where'd you find this?" Climbing down the ladder on the side of his boat, Pueo turned to Atomos with a beaming smile. He leaned toward the whale, picking at the barnacles stuck to its skin.

"I found it beached on the far side of the island. Isn't it a shame I couldn't have been there earlier to help it?" muttered Atomos somberly. "I wonder how old it was, or if it had any friends or a family."

"Must have been a very noble creature," whispered Pueo. "Atomos, you know what I love most about them? It's these bumps and scars along a whale's skin that make them so unique."

Atomos thought of his own scar, connecting his nose to his upper lip. He tried not to think about it often.

Pueo continued, "The native Hawaiians would've made these whale bones into tools for hunting. It was a rite of passage for young warriors. Actually, in most cases, they were only a few years older than you, Atomos." Atomos hung on every one of Pueo's words, anxiously nodding up and down. Pueo put his hand on the boy's shoulder. "Well, do you think it's time?"

"Really?" exclaimed Atomos.

"Go get my tools in the hut. What do you say?"

Atomos ran up to the toolshed behind their hut. He was so excited that he didn't think twice. He didn't expect to be going hunting for a few more years at least. This was going to be a great adventure! He might be strong, but a spear would make him fast—or, at least, faster. Atomos was quick to gather everything he needed from around the hut, excited by the prospect of being able to hunt while Pueo was away fishing or on his trips to the other islands to buy cooking supplies. Sometimes, when Pueo came back, he brought books and movies on discs called Blu-ray. It was old technology, but Atomos was captivated nonetheless. Neither of them knew how to surf the web, torrent or pirate a movie, nor freely stream anything at all.

That evening, they pulled a roasted pig that had been cooking all day out of the fire pit. Toasted and crispy, Atomos admired the steam escaping from its busted skin. Pueo cut into it with his knife while fragrant juices exploded from the pork's crispy exterior. As he lifted it, the pig's supple white meat fell right off the bone, which Pueo tossed into the fire alongside the fat.

"I've taught you a little bit about the traditions of Hawai'i, haven't I?" The stars glistened over Pueo's head. "I know you are not one of us by blood, Atomos. You're not Polynesian. But, nonetheless, there is a connection between all of us, here, on this earth, past, present, and future.

Fire isn't the only lifeblood of our culture, so is our food and our dances. In India, some say dancing started the universe. Fire and deadly vipers dance to demonstrate their mastery over death. Which reminds me, in ancient Greece, there was once an ancient healer, worshipped for using snake venom to bring a man back from the dead. His name was Asclepius, son of Apollo." Atomos was beginning to grow wary of these tall tales. How would knowing about dead people impact his life? "His mother was a beautiful, mortal woman."

"What was her name?"

"Her name was Coronis, with an *s* at the end, not Corona."

"Kronos?" questioned Atomos half-heartedly. Hadn't he heard that name before? "Wasn't he the Titan that ruled over the world after chaos?"

"Yes, that's right. He was the father of the gods."

"So, did none of the Titans survive?" asked Atomos.

"Oceanus did, I suppose. They never got him." Pueo tossed the pile of bones and gristle that had collected by his feet into the fire. "That's what they say about all Titans, though: they're unsinkable." Pueo laughed. "They weren't wrong. The ocean does control the weather, the climate, and the oxygen we breathe. We really do owe it everything."

After they'd finished the deboning, Atomos and Pueo took the pork to eat for dinner down on the boat. By then, it was so dark out that Atomos couldn't see where he walked, carrying the food.

"Atomos?" began Pueo. He was sitting with a mouthful of food. A propane light stood off to the side of the wooden table on board. "Did you remember to put a tarp over the fire pit?"

"No, I didn't," replied Atomos. "Maybe, I could—"

"Can you just go do it now?" interjected Pueo. "It's going to rain."

Atomos got to his feet and walked back to the fire pit. It wasn't going to rain. There hadn't been more than a handful of clouds all day. *It's no use arguing*, thought Atomos. He didn't want Pueo to do any of this work, not when he could do it so much easier himself. For this, Atomos thought he was very mature, more so than anyone else his age. However, in reality, Atomos knew almost nothing about any subject that required much thought. He dragged the tarp over to the dirt. When Atomos got back, he knew a lecture was waiting for him:

"Dirt is a commodity on this island, Atomos," began Pueo. Atomos had only just stepped through the doorway.

"I understand," replied Atomos with a sigh. "I—"

"I'm not done," continued Pueo, reassuring but stern. "There's a reason we take the tarp and put it over the dirt. It's to keep it all in one place."

"Absolutely," interjected Atomos again, nodding. "No, seriously, I get it. It's all about the dirt. You're right, always. The compost worm is the mightiest creature in the animal kingdom." Atomos had an extremely sarcastic tone. He didn't care. Pueo was always repeating himself. He felt well aware of anything and everything the fisherman could ever say. Atomos drooped his head, staring at his food. Pueo didn't like this reaction in the slightest.

"The reason our soil is such a commodity, Atomos, is because we live on a volcano." While Pueo spoke, Atomos grew visibly more perturbed by the second. Still, he remained silent. "Vegetation grows everywhere. You know as well as I. Digging in the soil must be a highly spiritual act; it must. You remember, according to our beliefs, every fire pit is a portal, a hole in the ground where spirits come in and out. As Hawaiians, we must cover these wounds whenever possible. In doing so, we remember Father Sky and Mother Earth's first baby, who was so badly deformed it came up as a bulb, and they buried it." Finally, Atomos paid attention to the story.

"Mother Earth cried over the grave site and out came a taro plant. Afterward, Father Sky and Mother Earth had another baby. The relationship goes like this: take care of the land; the land will take care of you. When I say 'you,' I really mean 'you.' We must treat the earth and the sky like family, Atomos. We must care for them forever."

Pueo got up after the two of them had finished eating in silence. He cleared off their plates. Atomos glanced over to the side of the boat where Pueo kept miscellaneous belongings and trophies from his travels; some he displayed behind a glass case. Closest to Atomos, four angry tiki statues stood, side by side. Each was unique, carved in bold and expressive shapes.

Their proportions were so dissimilar that some failed to even look human. Nobody had eyes or ears that large. In fact, one even looked like a cat.

"So, when the earth shakes," proposed Atomos, "you're telling me that's Mother Nature being loving?" He looked down at the ground between his bare, dirty feet and noticed Pueo's tackle box was open. Inside, he had leaders, swivels, sinkers, floats, rings, wire, snaps, beads, spoons, and blades. It was a tangled mess. Nothing was in order. The sticker on the side of the box bore the logo of a local commercial fishery that sometimes gave Pueo work. However, after all these years, the once green-and-blue sticker was almost entirely torn away.

"Exactly," said Pueo confidently, ignoring the doubt he heard in the boy's voice. "Mother Nature is the most loving then."

"What about when the sky blows winds and makes forty-foot waves?" continued Atomos. "What about when the forest catches fire or when a volcano erupts and covers an entire city? What about plagues? You're saying that isn't punishment? There's bombs that can kill millions."

"We live on this small island, far away from everyone else, for a very specific reason, Atomos. Out here, there is no escaping our fears. We are all we have; this is our reality. Everyone else can ignore their problems out there, but unless we plunge into a nuclear winter, we each have both the privilege and also the burden of always being alone with them. You know, I learned these lessons when I was not much older than you, Atomos."

Pueo exited the front area and went into the back room of the boat, where he slept, pushing past a large green cloth hung from the ceiling. Atomos heard Pueo rifling through his belongings. As he turned, his backside sent pots and pans crashing to the ground. Pueo turned back around and carried a large, hand-carved spear back through the kitchen. Without a word, he handed it over to Atomos. "This is yours now, Atomos. Tomorrow, we begin teaching you the ancient ways of spearfishing."

"Thanks, Pueo," responded Atomos, quick and short. He squinted and turned his head to the side. "Can I go now?"

"Yes, you can go, Atomos." As Atomos got up and started toward the door, however, Pueo continued, "I'll be gone tonight. A new customer paid my last-minute delivery charge. I won't be back until later tomorrow. Maybe next year, though, you could go with me. We could make some money together, just not quite yet. You understand, right?"

"Yeah, no worries. Aloha," shouted Atomos, already out the door. Never in his entire life had he ever been so sure of anything. Atomos desperately wanted nothing more than to explore the world. His island was so small. Surely, somewhere, there must be some semblance of humanity left. Death might be unavoidable, but it existed in a cycle, like water. After enough time, new life would spring from the soil, and so on, and so on. Even the disappearance of the Great Barrier Reef, which could no longer be seen from space, had its place in the universe. The end, Atomos knew, was just another beginning. *After all*, he thought, *what's Earth other than one big blue circle?* Why should he care what was on the horizon?

Pueo's ship sailed off into the night.

3
BELOW THE SURFACE

The sky was blue and the clouds were white the next day when Pueo returned; none carried rain as predicted. Atomos waited as Pueo dropped anchor, but then stepped back inside at once. Atomos had been waiting all day. What was another second? He'd spent half the morning dumping buckets of water on the bloodstained dock and scrubbing its boards. Blood drained off into the surf below; the remaining bits of its blubber, however, went to the birds. Some that remained landed on the boat's radio equipment, wretched and caked in sand.

Atomos was confused. *Why isn't Pueo getting off the boat?* The winds blew a bit stronger. The coconut trees shuffled their thousand leaves. The more he listened, the more they had to say—music in the chaos.

"Pueo? Are you there?" yelled Atomos.

Pueo was an average human. His most impressive traits were his creativity and determination. Nobody but him could amass such amazing collections, though it made sense why he'd grown so attached. In Pueo's own lifetime, the end of the Holocene and the dawning of the Age of

Aquarius, climate change had nearly wiped out all the world's supply of coral. They'd been one of the original beings of life. They brought structure to the planet. Humans brought peril. Still, in their infinite ingenuity, humans found a way to rectify the situation. All it took was a global food crisis for them to draw the world's attention to the oceans, albeit by artificial means. In the end, though, the science worked. Humanity won, or, at least, that's what they said. The coral *Statue of Reassurance* rode her chariot, triumphant, near what some call Queen Victoria's island and others deem Pig Island. Thanks to science and cold fusion, the planet was well protected from global warming, at least for the time being.

"Over here!" An arm jetted out the window. "I'm just grabbing something. Won't be a minute." Pueo's arm then retracted back inside. *What could possibly be holding him up?* Before Atomos had much longer to ponder this thought, Pueo came around the corner. In an instant, Atomos understood why the old man had taken his time. Pueo was holding his own spear. The engraving looked antique. "Aloha," Pueo said with unrivaled gusto. "Welcome to your first day of spearfish training! Are you ready to start?"

Pueo and Atomos paddled into calmer waters. Still, they were easily within reach of the reef. The fish would be somewhere along here, as long as there hadn't been any bleaching. Was that a speck of it there? The infamous bone-white coral. He didn't know—was it dead or alive? They kept paddling. A few rocks stuck out, here and there. Waves shifted on top of them. Atomos had grown accustomed to their dependable, steadfast rhythm. The push and pull of the ocean were incredibly powerful forces, moving around him, most of all below.

"Sorry I took so long today," began Pueo. "You should've seen the haul. Bloody mackerel! That fish I caught, Atomos. You'd've been proud. I shouldn't have gone out so far, though, maybe?"

"It's okay," replied Atomos. *Why is he apologizing?* "I'm just glad you're here now, to teach me everything." For once, he felt honest and happy with himself, but the worst lies are the ones you tell yourself.

"Okay, we're here," noted Pueo as he leaned back. He held up his spear and switched hands. "Hold my board." Pueo dove into the ocean. Water splashed everywhere. Atomos tried focusing on the shadow beneath the bubbling surf, but Pueo was nowhere to be seen. Atomos held Pueo's surfboard with his right hand. The other gripped his spear.

Suddenly, Pueo came up with a fish.

"That was wild!" shouted Atomos, impressed. The creature was bigger than Pueo's whole arm, shoulder and all. It was two-toned, like it had racing stripes, each a vibrant blue with yellow fins. Spikes protruded from its back half. "Can I go?" burst Atomos. "I'm ready. I swear!" He aimed to dive in that second, but Pueo held up his hand.

"First, Atomos, I want you to know, our strategy is to be as relaxed as we can get; that'll save oxygen. Before you get into the water, we're going to take a couple nice deep breaths. Then, you'll get in and, slowly, try to work your way to the bottom. Don't worry. I'll be here in case anything happens. Once you're there, make your movements even slower. Don't rush a thought, Atomos. Don't rush anything. Rushed or awkward movements will only push fish away from you. Remember that. When you see a fish swim by, every part of your body will start reacting all at once. You'll want to go faster and faster, but you won't be able to. Your excitement will expose you. Time slows down in the ocean. These things will be your enemy down below. Do you hear me?"

"I do." Atomos attempted to persuade Pueo with a nod. "Deep breaths. Stay calm. Don't overthink. If I can't get a fish," said Atomos, "I'm better off rethinking my strategy, coming back up, and working on my technique."

"Exactly. That's right. You got it. Think deep, don't sink."

Isn't that exactly what he said not to do? Atomos got off his board, wading in the water.

"Now, go on. I'll hold your board," suggested Pueo reassuringly. He leaned over, placing his hand palm down.

"All right, here goes nothing." Atomos took a deep breath, filling every corner of his lungs with precious air. Down he dove, headfirst. A jet of bubbles followed behind as he plunged deeper and deeper. He hoped to see a sea dragon. They were like seahorses but much more rare. Almost none had survived after losing the first round of coral. Three yellow, wide-eyed fish with flushed red faces swam alongside a long, gray stingray underneath his feet; or, Atomos was now considering, above his feet, seeing as how he was now upside down.

Atomos swam past a bed of coral. He thought they were rocks at first, but they weren't. Each structure was absolutely teeming with life. Living in and among the coral's little cracks and crevices were some of the most beautiful and lively beings Atomos figured had ever been seen. Underwater, even the lines between plants and animals seemed to shift and move. Coral was both. Symbiosis was embedded into its fibrous being. After understanding that duality, imagining the clownfish and sea anemone as anything other than one entity seemed impossible. A starfish sat on a rock and a red crab shuffled in the sand beside a purple coral plate, fanning out like the petals of a flower. Was that a mollusk? Atomos became entangled in bright-green sea kelp, dangling and drifting in the watery breeze. All of these creatures were just barely out of reach.

Salt water flooded into his mouth. Atomos hated the crude taste and rough texture of the ocean in the back of his throat. Atomos decided to return to the surface to catch his breath; however, no sooner did he turn toward the sky than a glimpse of a large bluish-black octopus in the distance caught his eye. Alas, it was too late for friends. The sky was darker. Only a small portion of the sun's curve was still above the water when Atomos surfaced, hacking and gasping for air. Somehow, it had stayed perfectly still there, suspended on the horizon. *Shouldn't it vanish?* Pueo wasn't surprised at all when Atomos came up empty-handed. He hadn't really expected a fish.

"Atomos," he began, "even though you caught no fish today, I commend you. You didn't fight the current or the surge. You learned how to deal with it. You used the ocean to your advantage." *How could he know?* "There's only one thing you're missing. But that's why I'm sure, beyond a shadow of a doubt, you'll catch a fish tomorrow."

"Tomorrow?" shouted Atomos.

"Now, Atomos, it's getting late. What do you say we call it a day?"

Atomos said nothing.

"We'll have a lot better luck tomorrow morning. You'll probably find traffic on the reef."

"Traffic?" questioned Atomos.

"If you're there at just the right time, you might even hear the morning chorus, purring, grunts, and groves. Wouldn't that be cool?"

Atomos said nothing. Together, the two of them paddled back to shore. After eating their catch over rice, Atomos went back to the hut to catch up on some reading while Pueo set sail. He was leaving the island once more for a last-minute fishing trip, under the cover of nightfall. There wasn't a single cloud in the sky. How rare. Atomos hopped up into his hammock. The shifting reflections of the moon and stars danced over the changing waters.

4

THE LONGEST STORM

Atomos spent the whole next day waiting for Pueo, but although time stretched on, the fisherman never did return. Lying in his hammock, reading *Frankenstein*, Atomos hung over the edge of the cliff, his feet crossed. Fluffy clouds moved across the horizon. The same gentle ocean breeze that guided them also cooled Atomos in the hot sun. He paid them no mind. How many hours had passed? Atomos set his book against his chest and gazed up at the sun, leaning his head back, approximately halfway across the sky. The bright neighboring stars peered through the clouds. Beams of light beckoned for him to forget himself, gesturing to join them in their radiant glory. Meanwhile, however, back on Earth, a fat raindrop splattered onto his forehead.

Closing his book with a sigh, Atomos crunched his abs and grabbed the tree trunk above. Mounting it with ease, he recovered his poise. Then, in a single bound, the boy jumped back onto the grassy hillside from which the tree sprouted. The grass was already wet from the drizzle, and Atomos slipped one or two feet when he landed. After walking through a patch of grass, his bare ankles were completely covered in mud. He wiped his feet with a towel taken from the surfboard stand, tossed the towel over a nearby lawn chair, and walked up the wooden steps into the hut. The storm raged on outside his window. Atomos lit a candle and set it on the foot of his bed. The electric bulbs on the ceiling fan overhead were far too dim to continue to read under.

The island grew darker and darker as rain fell from the heavens. Lightning flashed, sending bolts of electricity far across the sky. Earth-shattering thunder echoed in every direction. Fierce winds howled long into the night. This might've been the longest and fiercest storm Atomos had ever experienced. Although the noise of constant upheaval kept him awake, he was not afraid; or, at least, that's what Atomos told himself. Nothing made him afraid. Whatever the storm might bring, Atomos knew he could handle it. *Nature is a teacher*, he surmised. Its lessons were designed to be challenging.

Outside, Atomos heard a large snap and proceeding crash. Peering out the window, he saw that not only had the palm tree closest to their hut fallen in the ferocious winds, but its trunk had landed on the pigpen. Worse yet, the force from the fall had knocked over its gate, and all the livestock had been set free. One last boar, brother to the one they had slaughtered earlier that week, was running amuck in the muddy grass. *What happened to the other three? Where are the chickens?* Atomos ran outside to chase the pig. The black-and-white-spotted creature was too fast for Atomos and, especially in the rain, far too slippery, squealing and oinking. Whenever the pig changed directions, Atomos slipped and covered himself in mud, getting drenched from head to toe.

Before too much more of this chaos went on, the little four-legged devil made a critical error. The pig doomed itself by running over the fire pit, and Atomos tackled it to the ground, restraining it, but not before tearing a huge gash into the tarp, ripping it to shreds. As Atomos carried the pig back to its pen over his shoulder, the pit filled with rainwater. Loose dirt and mud ran down the hillside. There was nothing Atomos could do. He tied the pig to a post. Then, his next goal was to rebuild the pigpen, despite the maelstrom. Atomos plunged the metal stakes back into the ground, attempting as best he could not to slip in the mud. The rain felt warm, running down his jawline, falling on his neck and shoulders.

Despite the strong winds, thunder, and lightning, Atomos paced outside in the grass. The frigid air bit into his skin, but this didn't bother Atomos. He was too distracted. Rubble and debris from the fallen trees were scattered everywhere. The lawn chairs were nowhere to be found, although it was still very dark out. It was possible, Atomos considered, that he just couldn't see them in the thick bushes. He walked past his hammock and down to the dock. This encounter was the most horrific sight yet: the dock, or rather lack thereof, was shattered and almost entirely taken by the ocean's current. The tarp, the hammock, and the lawn chairs could all be replaced, but Pueo had built the dock himself. Atomos remembered those days clearly, although he must have only been five or six at the time.

Vicious waves crashed into the rocky shore. That night, once the storm had passed, Atomos walked to the top of the island in the moonlight, stopping only to see if there were any hopeful lights in the distance. There weren't.

The next morning, Atomos went for a walk around the island. He wanted to see for himself what other kinds of damage the storm had wrought. Plus, if Atomos were to see any of the other boars, he had his spear. As he walked around the beach, Atomos looked up and thought about the clouds in the sky above. They seemed a bit more ominous than usual, remnants of the chaos that had occurred. *Perhaps*, pondered Atomos, *they'll pass*. It was still early.

The sun had barely risen over the water. The morning star took its place. Nonetheless, the heat barreled down onto his back. Atomos followed his shadow, stretching out further than ever before. He half expected to see another whale as he turned the corner; however, like the other thousands of times he'd been here, there was nothing. Trash was still there, though, like always. Pollution wasn't going away. There was, however, always something interesting in the mess. This time, it was a haphazardly welded metal bike frame. Atomos gazed out to sea with a puzzled expression and then turned back toward the island. He noticed the trees on this side of the island were still mostly intact. It was hard for Atomos to tell, though. They were all so high up on the cliffside.

The waves pushed back and forth on shore, climbing up the wet sand, absorbing and erasing every footstep as Atomos walked. The drier sand, further from the water, covered his ankles and the tops of his feet. This, at least, was better than mud. The further Atomos journeyed, the more he began to reflect on all the past occasions he'd used this time to get away, to avoid Pueo. Atomos wanted to go back and wait. He decided to climb the cliffs and walk straight back through the jungle. He shook off the sand in between his toes. No doubt climbing the waterfall would be much easier this time around. When Atomos reached the waterfall, he found something in his path that defied any and all wildest expectations.

Saying Atomos was unprepared would be an understatement. This was not simply something he didn't expect; this was something Atomos had never seen nor imagined before: a real-life dragon!

THE FLOATING MOUNTAIN

5

The large, black eyes were intoxicating. Head to tail, the twenty-foot reptile was larger than any living thing Atomos had ever seen. Six bulky horns stuck up out of its scaly blue head. A snarling hiss and long blue tongue escaped its toothy jaws. Atomos could tell from the way the creature stood that it was desperately out of place on dry land. Despite being covered top to bottom in mud and sticks, the creature was uniquely majestic, vibrant, and monstrous, like the sea. Violently, the creature whipped its head back and forth in anger. Rearing back, letting out a deafening roar, the dragon then spread its twenty-foot wings. Atomos was petrified. He had never once thought any kind of dragon was real, especially not ones that lived in the sea.

Atomos held up his spear. He didn't want to hurt the creature, but if that's what it came down to, he would. Atomos inched closer, shuffling through the shallow water. The creature's four flippers were powered by muscles that, alone, were larger than his entire body. The creature struggled desperately to maneuver through the landscape. Twice, it attempted to stand; each time, however, it slipped and fell under its own weight. The root of the problem was a large tree branch, broken off on each side, protruding from the creature's front leg. The dragon gnawed at the wound. Seeing this, Atomos lost all doubt and went in. With his incredible strength, he lifted the creature.

At first, the creature resisted, crying out, even attempting to bite Atomos with its razor-sharp, gator-like teeth. But Atomos used his spear to cut the tree branch out, and the creature whimpered and fell limp. Atomos walked it out into the ocean. He stepped over stones and logs, most of which broke under their tremendous combined weight. Still, inch by inch, he brought the creature closer to its home. Mud that had dried on the creature washed down his back. Atomos pushed on, further into the shallows. With every step, his legs sank deeper into the sand. Once he was up to his waistline in muddy water, the creature suddenly leaped from his arms and swam away. Atomos was happy. He'd helped save a life. Still, overall, the encounter made him sad. Once again, he was alone. He hoped the monster wasn't hurt. Atomos went back to the hut and collected wood as he walked. He spent the whole rest of the day gathering supplies to rebuild the dock before Pueo returned.

After a week of waiting on the mountaintop, hoping to see a light in the distance, Atomos awoke one morning in a haze. He was beginning to think he'd never see Pueo or the dragon again. Peering out his window, Atomos noticed a chilling white mist hanging over the ocean. But this light did not appear so thick as to drown out the shining morning star. He walked down the small hill, onto the rocks, and out into the water. His bare feet were cold, but Atomos kept on. His demeanor was ghostly and calm. A sliver of sunlight rose over the waves. Water splashed up against his legs and waist. Atomos pushed on, not caring where the tide took him. He couldn't feel anything, or at least not currently. In front of him, everything waited in suspense; behind him, the world stopped in his wake. The universe wasn't supposed to be like this. Nobody was meant to be so alone. The water was up to his neck. He couldn't touch below.

Suddenly, a colossal wave plunged toward Atomos. Worse yet,

the swell carried a gigantic palm tree, swinging for his head. Atomos immediately came to his senses. His skin might be uncuttable, but a tree this large would knock him out like a light.

Atomos dove under the water, avoiding the tree's thick body by mere inches. Turning around and opening his eyes once again, Atomos reached out and took hold of the trunk. He snapped the wood in half, attempting to make a makeshift vessel to float on. Lifting his torso over the board and wrapping his legs tight around it, Atomos was able to steady himself for a moment before another wave came tumbling down on top of him. Its crushing weight tossed Atomos out into the open ocean, rending what was left of his floating branch to splinters.

Atomos tumbled and turned over again and again in the swell. Water slammed against his chest, even into his lungs. Never before had his superhuman strength felt so useless. However, just as Atomos was beginning to abandon all hope of surviving this encounter with Mother Nature, one of her most curious instruments came from the depths to save him. The sea dragon! As blue and radiant as the sea, she appeared like something out of a vision. The sun shone behind her round, serpentlike head. Her scaly, blue skin shimmered in the sunlight. Atomos was mesmerized as the dragon turned her head, hovering over his own. A drizzle of clear water dripped down onto his chest. Atomos reached his arm out toward her cheek. She leaned into his touch.

"I couldn't even see you!"

Although she'd saved him from down below, among the coral, she didn't seem to belong to that world either. All the energy of a summer's day filled her black eyes, like lightning in a bottle. Why wasn't the sky nearly as blue as the scales along her neck? Was the sun no longer as yellow? Cobalt and indigo were each too dark to describe her hue. Sapphire was too violet; turquoise too green. "Tell me, how do you like the name Azure?"

She nodded.

He was astounded by her intellect. "Awesome!"

Atomos decided shortly afterward to leave the island in search of Pueo or, perhaps, in search of something greater. The rest of the world couldn't be as bad as Pueo had said it was. Atomos had never left the island before, but now anything was possible. Each day the sun set, but the horizon never changed. Pueo would never return; that was that. Armed with only a spear and some cargo shorts, Atomos and Azure set sail. The ocean was calm. There was hardly a wave. Still, this was the open ocean. Sink or swim, that was it for him. He had to survive on his own. Atomos lifted his hand to his brow, gazing beyond the horizon, pondering his not-so-distant future. When would he find his new world?

Hours went by. Floating through the ocean on Azure's back was tiring work, almost as much as looking for anything other than water in any direction. The sun beat down. Atomos wiped his brow. *How did Pueo navigate so easily?* All Atomos understood was the angle of the sun. Pueo knew so much more. His parents were locals, having raised him in the early part of the twenty-first century. To them, however, the practice of tourism wasn't far from exploitation. Politics ruled everything in Hawai'i.

Water splashed on both sides of Azure's face and neck as she dodged oncoming waves. Her shimmering blue limbs propelled them forward through the water, never rising more than a few feet above the surface. Meanwhile, Azure kept her wings tucked firmly against her back. Atomos had never seen her fly. Perhaps they were relics of her ancient ancestors, like an appendix.

In the distance, a pair of gray tails burst up out of the ocean water. Incredible! There was a big one and a little one. Atomos wondered if they were a pod looking for the beached whale he'd found. Atomos eyed his bone spear. Perhaps he wasn't meant to be a great fisherman. Perhaps he was a fluke. From the shape and size of their tail fins, though, there was no way these two were the same species. Actually, they were humpbacks. Ocean spray cascaded down their coarse calluses. Water droplets danced on their backs. Atomos thought of Pueo. The whales were like the two of them. The last moments they'd spent together they spent hunting.

Azure swam on. More hours passed. Atomos saw a dolphin and even a rainbow. Nothing, however, made him more excited than spotting a speck of an island out of nowhere. No, this wasn't an island. This was a mountain! Furthermore, while the mountain grew taller, it also grew darker. Despite the object's ominous presence, Azure bounded forward, faster than ever, barreling across the water. She was so confident.

The mountain was nearly black and very tall, so high up that Atomos couldn't see the top; all he could see was its wide base. Azure seized back. Did she want them to leave? No, it was the object. The mountain, it was moving! Swaying back and forth, the towering structure pointed sharply out of the sea. Momentous waves pushed and pulled, back and forth, exposing huge, gaping caves underneath its base. Again and again, the waves receded and crashed violently against the black cliffside. Atomos speculated, *Perhaps it is even bigger below the surface, like an iceberg.*

Azure brought Atomos as close as she could to the floating mountain, extending her head and neck high and far forward for him. From between her shoulder blades where he usually sat, Atomos climbed along her spikes and leaped off her head. He grabbed hold of the rocky cliffside. Rubble and debris crumbled underneath the weight of his body, but quickly, he found his grip. He was surprised to find the shining black rock was cold to the touch. Everywhere he looked, its surface was covered in a layer of frost. This was remarkable. Atomos had never seen so much ice outside of an icebox. He'd always thought that ice was supposed to be white. Still, he wasn't going to let a little cold ruin his adventure. Atomos pushed on. Below, Azure waited by the base of the mysterious black mountain.

Climbing up the iceberg was taking far longer than anticipated. Each time he ascended twenty feet, forty more seemed to rise above him. Atomos flinched when a part of the cliff broke off like an icicle and plummeted down to the water. He focused his vision. He was already hundreds of feet in the air. This, too, was a brand new experience. The highest tree on his island might've been half this far up. Shattered ice crystals fell into the water, making a series of tiny splashes below, or at least that's how it sounded. The strange ice wasn't sinking. Instead, Azure saw each get caught into a swell and then crash back into the side of the mountain, sticking in place like a magnet. *But why would ice act like graphite? Isn't it made from mostly hydrogen?*

Atomos stood atop a ledge, his bare feet freezing. He turned and scanned the wide-open ocean. In the distance, four figures rose out of the sea. *Submarines?* As they drew in closer, it was clear that all of them were sea dragons too; however, they were larger than Azure. From a distance, the design of their riders' armor resembled mounted samurai. The only difference was that the fierce warriors wore silver and carried gold tridents. Azure was panicked. Her gills violently slapped the water as she dove below. The four knights encircled her.

Atomos screamed from atop the cliff, "Hey! Leave her alone!" Had they heard him in the slightest? What was he going to do? The riders threw their nets around her body and turned away from the mountain. Despite her loud roar and violent seizing, they continued on. Atomos took a deep breath. He jumped. Speeding toward the surface of the water in a free fall, Atomos let go of his spear. Waving his arms above his head, he screamed the whole way down.

Furthest back in the group, the red dragon and its rider turned just in time to see the leap of faith. Atomos pointed his feet together, plunging nearly fifteen feet into the freezing water before coming back up to the surface. Unfortunately, however, his spear did not float.

Opening his eyes, cold water dripping through his hair, Atomos saw a trident pointed directly at his neck, held by the golden samurai. How minatory. This menace, however, was the least of his fears. The dragons in front of him were much more captivating. One was black, the other red, although both their eyes were entirely black, like Azure's. Their breath was heavy and warm. Their teeth looked razor sharp and white, although their mouths were the same color as their scales, inside and out. The knight who rode the black dragon was the one pointing his trident at Atomos. He was big and burly, with a strong jawline and long, strange, catlike ears sticking out of his helmet. All of them had these same curious ears, Atomos noticed. But Atomos was most absorbed by the black dragon's head, sporting four large, black horns.

The other warrior eyed Atomos intently. Meanwhile, his red dragon jerked its long neck back and forth, distracted. His own trident lay back against his shoulder as he took off his helmet to reveal long, silver hair. A single scar rested above his eyebrow. *Neither of them could be more than four or five years older than me,* thought Atomos.

"Who are you? Why are you here?" demanded the brawny warrior.

"I'm Atomos," answered the boy, too busy keeping afloat to bother with a lengthy reply. Atomos reached up toward the trident, not afraid of its sharp points whatsoever. He grabbed on with both hands. "Mind giving me a hand, mate?"

"Give me one good reason why I shouldn't kill you right now." The trident didn't budge. The samurai's black dragon puffed a hot gust of air, growling. If they weren't human, how'd they know English? These aliens didn't have the internet, did they? Atomos had never felt more out of the loop.

"C'mon, Oberon. Help him up," insisted the longer-haired warrior. His nose was long and his voice was unexpectedly deep. "Don't you want to know how much he knows?" The red dragon's tongue shot out of its mouth, red and forked. It cleaned its beard and muzzle.

"Don't you see his clothes? He's human," said Oberon.

"He has a dragon," replied his counterpart.

"Exactly, Zagreus, that's what—"

"This is a mystery, Oberon. Please. Don't deny me this," snapped Zagreus. Oberon lifted his trident, pulling Atomos out of the water, and set him on a ledge on the base of the mountain. He removed his helmet, revealing short, spiky, black hair.

"Now, I'll ask you once more," demanded Oberon, clenching his fist. "How did you come to have a dragon?"

Atomos shivered in the cold, clinging to the iceberg for dear life as the waves continued to smash against him. Behind them, the other two samurai were attempting to hold Azure steady. Suddenly, her head and neck broke free. Their dragons moved swiftly, blocking his sight. Azure roared. Over her voice, he heard the warriors shout at each other, encircling her once more.

"Grab her!" one yelled.

"I am!" screamed the other.

Atomos could tell by the pitch of their voices that they were women. The purple dragon had an extremely large tail and black eyes, like the others, but the other knight rode a white dragon with red eyes. Atomos was frantic. He couldn't lose Azure, his only friend—not here, in the middle of the Pacific Ocean, especially not so soon after finding her. He couldn't swim back.

"She came to me," shouted Atomos. "I helped her back to health after the big storm. I didn't know she would take me to your island. You've got to believe me. I've never even heard of this place!"

"This island isn't ours, you sniveling idiot."

Atomos recoiled as Oberon shoved his trident back in his face. The other two warriors took off their helmets as well. Like the boys, the girls were mere teenagers. They were also noticeably distinct. The black-haired girl was much more muscular than the silver-haired girl in a way that Atomos thought was extremely reminiscent of their boyish counterparts. Her eyebrows were also thick and her hair was curly.

"You can ride her?" gasped the silver-haired girl on top of the white dragon. The black-haired girl sat by with a silent, judgmental expression. She, too, was easy on the eyes. Actually, all of the knights had the same dark-indigo eyes. Her purple dragon turned its majestic head.

"Yes, I can," replied Atomos tentatively.

"If you can ride dragons, you must come with us. Absolutely," she added, gleeful. Her red-eyed albino dragon shook its head side to side in the wind.

"What are you saying?" objected Oberon. "You're all friendly with humans now? Am I the only one who sees what's really going on here?"

"Where are all you from?" asked Atomos, realizing the peculiar way Oberon said *humans*.

The long-haired warrior spoke up in his deep, raspy voice. "This is my sister, Venus," he announced, gesturing to the silver-haired girl on the albino dragon. "I'm Zagreus, the first Dionysian. You've met Oberon. That's his sister, Titania, over there. She doesn't talk." Titania looked away as Zagreus introduced her, clearly upset that her name had even been mentioned. Venus removed the nets restraining Azure. As soon as she was free, Azure swam over to Atomos, rescuing him from the cold, slippery cliffside.

"We are the guardians of the Gyre," said Venus softly. "Separate, we are like the seasons. Together—"

"We protect the secret," interrupted Oberon.

"What secret?" asked Atomos. Everyone was silent, sitting under the shadow of the black mountain. Their dragons turned to look at one another. Atomos stared at the strange teenagers, confused.

"The Gyre," replied Zagreus, slowly. "It's also known to your kind as the Isle of Immortals, the home of all dragons." Atomos was stunned. Until a little over a week ago, he'd thought dragons were a myth. Now, supposedly, there was a whole civilization dedicated to keeping them a secret? With these four in front of him, each with black eyes and catlike ears, an island of dragons like Azure was hard to deny.

"So, what exactly is a Gyre?"

"The Gyre," chirped Venus, "is a water structure. It facilitates prayer, meditation, and healing: mind and body. Some say it is where one must go to find their true selves."

"So, this island—"

"No. Aren't you listening?" shouted Oberon. "I mean, how dumb do you have to be?" His dragon dipped its head in the water and then violently whipped its black horns back, splashing Atomos in the face. Oberon shook his head with scorn and contempt.

"What?" asked Atomos, unfazed.

"This is your island, not ours," continued the samurai harshly. "Look there, behind you. That's the work of human hands." Atomos turned and gazed where Oberon was pointing. "See all those jagged edges and the sporadic protrusions? They're murder weapons, every one of them—ask the fish." Atomos saw thousands of them. "The history of humanity is all happening right here, right now. Don't you forget, it's your future, too, human." A pulsating vein protruded from his forehead.

"All right, Oberon, that's enough," insisted Zagreus. "We'll take him with us to the Isle of Immortals, and the council will decide if he can stay. Unless you have some sort of problem with the council?"

Oberon huffed but said nothing. After that, he refused to look Atomos in the eyes. That was fine. Atomos was relieved more than he was offended. Why should he care if they insulted humans? He was just glad to be on Azure's back again.

Riding on the backs of their five dragons, they swam together in unison, leaving the mysterious floating mountain in their wake. The sun drifted low in the sky as they rode. As time passed, Atomos grew more unsure about what he was going to do. Part of him wanted to continue searching for Pueo, but the guardians would surely take Azure from him if he tried anything. Had he truly set out to find Pueo, though? Hadn't he set out trying to find the truth about humanity? Well, maybe he had. Maybe he'd already found it. Who knew?

While Zagreus and Oberon talked up front, Atomos leaned over to Venus, riding on her white-scaled, red-eyed dragon.

"Venus?" Atomos asked. "Why did Oberon say the floating mountain represented humanity? I didn't see any humans."

She'd been hoping someone else might do the explaining for her. Her dragon stretched its right wing over the water on the far side from Atomos. After removing her helmet with a delicate sigh, she began her long-winded story:

"For the past two hundred years or more, humans have been disposing of their unwanted plastic in the ocean—out of sight, out of mind. The island they call the Pacific Trash Vortex is ten times larger than the Great Barrier Reef. I call it what it is: Trash Island. Can you imagine? It's not like the Gyre produces any plastic." Suddenly, Venus remembered who she was talking to. "That's interesting you call it a mountain, though," she concluded. "You're right, of course. It's very big."

"The future of the human race," breathed Atomos, "is choking." He thought back to all the times he'd collected trash on the beach. All the offenders were commonplace items: plastic bags, six-pack holders, straws.

Nothing, however, could've prepared him for such a monstrosity. The sheer size was unfathomable. Even now, he still couldn't process it. "But, Venus, there's one thing I still don't understand: why was it cold?"

"That was the humans, too," she countered. "I don't know how they did it, just that these ships came in with some sort of chemical. After they were done, everything solid was fused together, turning black—even the wildlife." Atomos glanced at Titania to see if she was listening. She wasn't, or at least she was good at pretending not to care.

"Venus," resumed Atomos, "one last question: how do you find the Isle of Immortals in the dark?" The sun was completely gone, although its pinkish-orange afterglow still donned the evening sky. Azure, however, had darkened to a midnight blue.

"We follow the stars," answered Venus.

"We're here," shouted Zagreus from up front, loud and clear.

"What?" squawked Atomos. The guardians stopped and turned to face each other. Atomos gazed at everyone, confounded. He couldn't see any island at all. Everything was dark. A few stars speckled the wide-open ocean. The light danced here and there. Where had they taken him?

The dragons gathered in a circle. Suddenly, Oberon spoke. "Are we seriously taking this human to the Gyre?" He looked around, upset that this offended none of the others. "Well, then, Guardians, I suppose if you believe this is for the good of all, the beginning of a new era, we shall find out, won't we?" Oberon inspected Atomos intently. "Don't choke, human," he added. Then, Oberon put on his silver-and-gold helmet. His monstrous black dragon dove down into the deep blue. Titania and her violet dragon dove down after.

Zagreus glanced at Venus on her albino dragon. "Can you handle this?" he asked, obviously referring to Atomos; this offended Atomos.

"Yeah. Definitely, no worries. You go on without me," replied Venus. Her brother plummeted into the depths below. Was he supposed to follow them? How deep were they going? When were they coming back? Atomos didn't have time to ask any of these questions. Before he could get anything out, Venus took her helmet and threw it into his lap. "Put it on," she insisted. Then, the silver-haired knight delicately caressed her dragon's head. She whispered under her breath, "Are you ready to be home, Vulcan?"

"Is this going to help me breathe underwater?" asked Atomos, not listening.

"Nope." She smiled.

"No?"

"All it does is help you see. But trust me, you're going to need that helmet more than me. Now, c'mon, stay low." Venus gestured to Azure. "I hope you can hold your breath." She plunged down below like the others. Atomos was alone. This was his moment to run away, to escape with Azure into the night. Atomos truly considered it for a moment, but then, images of dragons entered his mind. Black, white, red, blue, purple—how many more were there? Atomos took a deep breath, the deepest he'd ever taken in his life. He leaned forward, preparing for a nosedive. What secrets waited in the deep?

6

JOURNEY TO ATLANTIS

Atomos put on the mysterious golden helmet just as his head hit the water. Azure was glowing! He thought the Isle of Immortals was an ancient civilization, but judging by the helmet, it was clear their technology was far superior to even the richest of humans. A glow emanated from his forearms. The guardians, though very small and far away, were bright and blue. Atomos was perplexed. Weren't there fish out here in the open ocean? Where were they?

Azure plunged ever deeper, swimming faster downward. The pull of the water felt immense around him. His neck, shoulders, and chest were all still bare, unlike the guardians. Venus and Zagreus rode in front— or, rather, below. The pitch-black water was disorienting. Bubbles flew everywhere. Some were pink, others purple. *Not a shred of light could have made it this far,* thought Atomos, *even in the peak of daytime.* How was he seeing all these colors? Was this illumination how he saw in his dreams? Suddenly, an uneasy weightlessness came over him. He felt light-headed. How long had he been holding his breath? His mind raced. How deep was he? How fast were they going? Had he been too focused on not being relaxed to take a moment and relax? Azure wasn't going to let him fall off, would she?

Atomos struggled. His breath-hold diminished by the second. However, in the distance, he began to make out a distant shape: a dancing black figure squirming in front of a giant blue light. Unlike the bubbles, this luminescence had no discernible shape or direction. The group swam closer and closer until, eventually, Atomos saw the shadow darting away from the light source. As Atomos intently focused upon the revelation, he saw that it wasn't simply a light there in front of him but a glowing temple.

Oberon was the first to arrive. His fierce four-horned dragon mounted the building's incandescent steps. Unlike the other dragons, Atomos could barely see the black beast in the darkness, but its glimmering scales gave it away. Oberon slid off the black sea beast. He pointed his trident at the huge, dark shadow above him.

Atomos joined Oberon and the others at the base of the steps. The temple seemed to be alive. He wouldn't think it possible, but the heat and light radiating from it felt almost present. Atomos wasn't sure whether the intensity of the tinge refracting around him was magnified by the temple itself or the helmet's visor, but at the same time, he didn't want to take it off and find out. Venus, however, still wore none. She didn't need to. Sliding off her albino dragon, she joined the others. Atomos awkwardly attempted the same.

The shadowy creature seemed less than fifty feet above them. Atomos saw the creature's terrifying limbs, reaching in every direction, sliding up the exterior of the luminous architecture. All assortments of sea life in and among the kelp darted away from the monster's slimy suction cups. Could the little turtle or the dolphin ever have made it this far? Perhaps they would've known to stay away. From the way the algae grew, in endless circles popping up here and there, Atomos was certain the monster must've been living here for decades, maybe longer.

Venus pointed toward the top of the stairs, signaling for him to follow her. Meanwhile, the five dragons swam toward the shadowy figure above.

Swimming past the algae-ridden columns and up the glowing steps, Atomos saw a long yellow-and-white hallway. More columns lay on each side. At the very end, maybe forty feet from him, a shining blue door seemed to beckon him. Strangely enough, he even heard it calling. It sounded almost like a tiny cry. How could he hear this? Venus put her hands up to his face, taking back the golden helmet she'd given him.

After placing the helmet under her arm, she smiled and lifted her other hand, wrapping it around her neck. Opening her mouth wide, bulging her eyes, she pretended to choke. Breathing was no joke to him. Atomos swam as fast as he could to the end of the hallway. He felt his heart beating violently through his entire body. He swam up to the door, which turned out not to be a door at all. Instead, where a door should be, a large gleaming sphere spun in a mad frenzy. Atomos stuck his hand into the curious void. In went his entire arm. An intense pressure tugged against his skin, almost like a whirlpool. The only difference was, on the other side, his fingers felt air. The wall of water must be a few inches thick. Atomos kicked aggressively. His head and his shoulders burst through the spiraling portal. He fell to the ground, landing on his back, and rolled around on the dry, white stones, gasping for air.

Back on his feet, Atomos coughed up more water. How could there be air trapped down here, so far under the surface? He scanned the circular room, surrounded by the spiraling, blue whirlpool. A beautiful yet simple fountain sprouted from the stone altar in the center of the room. One single leg and bowl held up a small pool of still water. Etchings in some strange language Atomos had never seen before decorated the fountain, engraved in gold. Perhaps they were elvish? He thought it best not to even try and read them. Four times, the whirlpool violently ruptured, and each time, one of the four guardians passed through the doorway, entering with ease. None had suffered like Atomos, it seemed. All four carried their dripping tridents, proudly landing on their feet. Zagreus lifted his own above his shoulders, yawning. Then, he placed it back on the ground and leaned upon it. Venus shook her silver hair.

"What are those engravings?" asked Atomos. "I've never seen—"

"That language is forbidden in the Gyre," yelled Oberon. "We do not speak it. We do not speak of it! Do you understand?"

"Okay, okay," laughed Atomos. "I'll make a mental note of that. It's just I—I still have a lot to get to know about your world. Well, anyway, did you just kill that giant squid?" Enthused, Atomos glanced around, having finally caught his breath.

"That giant squid," responded Oberon, quickly taking off his own helmet and stepping up to Atomos, "is the reason your disgusting, pathetic, soul-sucking species hasn't destroyed these sacred grounds. You probably don't even know what I'm talking about." As Oberon turned and walked around the fountain, he savagely added, "Actually, when we were outside, I thought he looked pretty hungry. Maybe he wants a snack."

"Hey, Oberon," said Zagreus. "Stop giving the kid such a hard time. He can't help that he's human. How could he have any clue what he just saw?"

Atomos appreciated the thought, but why did Zagreus call him a kid? These so-called guardians were only two or three years older than him at most. And so what? Why'd it matter how old he was? They weren't going to school, were they? What school would there be in the middle of the ocean? Atomos looked at the girls to see if they cared if he was younger.

Meanwhile, Zagreus continued speaking directly to Atomos. "You've heard of dragons, kid, but have you ever heard of Atlantean rings?" Zagreus removed his gold-plated gloves to reveal a green ring. The other guardians did the same and gathered around the fountain. Atomos noticed Oberon was missing a finger. "Hold on," Zagreus warned. He turned to Atomos. "I'm just now realizing, I don't remember your name." Zagreus scanned the room. "Do any of you remember?"

Oberon stuck his nose up into the air, puffing wind through it obnoxiously. He clearly had no interest in such trivial matters. Titania had nothing to say either. She just shrugged and looked away. Venus surveyed Atomos with wide eyes. With a smile that couldn't have been much more than surface deep, she mouthed the words, *I am sorry.*

"My name is Atomos."

"Atomos, huh?" responded Zagreus "I've never heard it before. Have you, Venus?"

"Nope," she acknowledged, smiling. "But I like it."

"Are you named after anyone important?" questioned Zagreus. "Does Atomos mean 'Son of Adam' in your culture?"

"No," answered Atomos.

"Enough. Get on with it, Z," demanded Oberon in his characteristically brash tone. "Green rings get you to the Gyre. Gold rings get you back. What's so complicated?" He glared at Atomos.

"Gold rings?" muttered Atomos. Then, speaking up, he asked the group, "Well, how will I get there? I don't have a ring at all."

With a smile and a glimmer in her eye, Venus took his hand. "Lucky for you, Atomos, you're with us." Each of the four guardians stuck their hands into the still water and pointed their ringed fingers down to the bottom of the fountain. Unlike the ornate carvings that encircled the outside of the bowl, the inside resembled the jagged and rocky surface of Mars or the moon. *Or perhaps*, Atomos considered, *it is the ocean floor.*

Atomos felt a sharp impact hit him square in the chest. His hands, elbows, and knees had all fallen into a pit of sand. Atomos got up and wiped the sand from his face and eyes. He was on a beach, all alone. There was no sign of anyone anywhere. Palm trees and grassy hills stretched out far in front of him. Closer, tall rocky cliffs reminded him of home, Pueo, and the whale. Turning in each direction, Atomos discovered that there were no buildings, no animals, not a single lonely soul anywhere. Where were the guardians? Where was Azure? Was he dreaming? When would he stop? The tide washed away his trail of footprints as Atomos walked along the beach, trying to work out exactly where on earth he was. There was something curious about the way the trees grew. On the island and everywhere else in the world, vegetation sprouted toward the sky. Rocks and stones couldn't hold them back, but Atomos had never seen so many growing off a rocky cliffside. Some even pointed straight down. No way they'd hold his hammock. No matter, anyway. He had a feeling he wouldn't be reading much. Shade was almost as hard to come by as free time.

Atomos gazed even further up, shocked by what he saw. The sky was bright, but the sun was absent. Where was it? No matter where he looked, Atomos saw nothing—no moon, no stars in the sky, nothing. Instead, the sky had long blue and white stripes, like ripples; although, as far as Atomos could tell, these were not clouds. Nowhere was there even a single cloud. Atomos squinted. His sights set upon the blue horizon, shifting and moving in the light. As far out as he could see, the edge of the Gyre appeared almost as if a huge wave was rising out of the ocean. Where did it end? Although he waited, watching the horizon intently for quite some time, the wave in the distance never moved closer. Atomos turned inland. Sand was still stuck to his chest.

Ascending a grassy hillside, no section trimmed or cut back, Atomos saw tall, wild bushes scattered along the hills. As he meandered along a lazy stream, he wiped off the remaining wet sand stuck to his legs and trunks. Meanwhile, unbeknownst to him, the shadow of a monstrous figure loomed in the distance, just beyond the surface of the enormous, all-encompassing wave. Just as quickly as it appeared, the shadow disappeared. Atomos peeked over his shoulder, having felt the light shifting behind him, but it was too late. He saw nothing.

Following a stream that flowed from the beach through the grassy hills and into a luscious, green forest, Atomos walked faster and faster. He was anxious to know where he was, almost as anxious as he was to get his hands on a gold ring. Atomos needed Azure if he was going to get back to Pueo. There was that and the fact that, in all honesty, he missed her. Atomos traveled along the riverbank, passing tree after tree through the thick tropics, before coming to a fork in the stream. Which avenue would get him back on the path to civilization? Atomos stood there for a long while, unable to make up his mind.

"Hey there, Adam," yelled Venus from behind, floating up the river with Zagreus in a canoe. "We were just in the neighborhood. Need a ride?" she asked cheerfully. Each of them still wore their armor but had lost their tridents and headwear. Instead, Zagreus had a paddle.

"Couldn't have come at a better time," said Atomos, waving. He climbed into the canoe, sliding in the middle seat between brother and sister. "I had no idea where I was going." He brushed the sand off his chest into the runoff below. "Or is it ideas? Either way—"

"Either way, we're glad you're here," interrupted Venus. Zagreus pushed off from the bank begrudgingly, paddling upstream.

"Good," replied Atomos with a timid smile, "but where exactly is here?"

"Welcome to the Isle of Immortals," said the girl cheerfully. "You are now one of very few to have ever walked on the bottom of the ocean."

"The bottom of the ocean?" exclaimed Atomos. He then paused and thought a moment. Zagreus just kept paddling onward. "So, this is a Gyre?" he remarked, mesmerized. Zagreus paddled onward.

"Yes, Adam, this is the Gyre," she answered.

"My name's Atomos."

"Like the atmosphere?"

"I'd like it a little more if I knew what a Gyre was," replied Atomos, oblivious.

Venus smiled. "Imagine the deepest, darkest place on earth, somewhere completely hidden from everyone forever. This is the Gyre; this is the eye of the storm."

"The bottom of the ocean?" he guessed.

"The Pacific Ocean," she specified. Atomos still felt unconvinced. Wouldn't the Atlantic be just as deep? Well, perhaps that wouldn't be the best hiding place for a group of people called Atlanteans. "Many choose to sit quietly and soak in the surroundings once they get to the Isle of Immortals," continued Venus. "You might call it meditation or prayer. Everyone experiences the Gyre's energy in their own way. It all depends on your sensitivity."

"What's there to be so sensitive about?"

"The Gyre, silly," replied Venus, twirling her fingers through her bright hair. "We're basically living inside a waterfall. The particles collide and produce tasteless, odorless mist molecules that relieve stress, fight depression, release tension, increase energy, and boost alertness. Forget about allergens and viruses and bad skin. I mean, they're called negative ions, but don't you just love them?" She winked. Meanwhile, Zagreus threw up his hood, covering his scar.

"After what Oberon said to me," muttered Atomos cautiously, "I wasn't sure if I could trust you." Although he'd always been insensitive on the outside, on the inside, there was no telling. Emotions were his weakness.

"Trust us?" she giggled. "Isn't it a given?"

"Given what? How could I after what you did? You wanted to throw me to the squid!"

"Well, that was then. What about now?" she prodded.

"Now, I realize, I don't have any other options." They all laughed. Quickly, though, Atomos cut in. "How about those rings, Zagreus? Do you know where I could find one?" Zagreus stared at Atomos with a mild annoyance. For half a second, the canoe drifted back downstream.

"Why do you think we're here, Atomos?" He began paddling again. "We all want a golden ring. Even without the games, though, we'd still be fighting over them. Life is unreal down here; death is uncertain. In the end, though, there's no escaping either. Look around. Everything about this place lacks the inspiration of your world. It lacks planning." Atomos looked around. The grass beside the stream was covered in dew; that much, at least, was the same.

"What are you getting at, Zagreus?" his sister asked. "The ancient Atlanteans forged this place to protect their technology."

"The Gyre is like everything else." Zagreus sighed, deeply, "It begins and ends in chaos. But, honestly, I don't consider it natural. Listen to me. I won't say it again. No cult, nor order of knights, will change my mind."

"The knights keep the peace. That's all I care about. Look at the chaos on the surface. You don't want to bring that here, do you, brother?" She pursed her lips and shook her silvery hair, smiling coyly.

"The Gyre is unbinding, as I see it." Atomos had no clue what was going on and so thought it best not to get involved. Soon, however, Zagreus began again. "You shouldn't judge Oberon harshly, Atomos.

You don't know his past. You don't know what he's been through. King Poseidon, the drowned Telchine, the Gyre's first immortal, well, that was his great-great-great-great-grandfather."

"Who?" questioned Atomos. "Poseidon? Like the Greek god? Are you guys Greek? Is that what this is? I thought we were in the Pacific."

"We are older than the Greeks, Atomos. Over three thousand years ago, the old king entered into a large, long-since-forgotten war with the surface world. He lost." Zagreus lost his usual sarcastic undertone. "Our civilization was destroyed. The most precious of our artifacts sank beneath the waves."

"But the temple I saw . . ." exclaimed Atomos.

"Four walls and a roof," countered Zagreus. "A single artifact from a once-great civilization; still, a portal. The ancient Atlanteans wanted someplace safe, so they hid everything in the Gyre." He sighed. "Why else leave us a single stone temple instead of a whole city?"

"They were jealous of our technology," added Venus. "Why can't humans understand? Teleportation and immortality would be too much for them. Nevertheless, in their endless greed, they won. We lost."

Zagreus paddled as he preached, pushing against the stream. "Power separated us before, but now, there's so much more." Did he mean more power or more separation? "Hundreds of miles of ocean water exist between our worlds. Still, despite these vast barriers, I have seen your world, human. I know your idea of humanity. Now, of course, I won't be as upfront about it as Oberon, but your people's crimes won't go unpunished, Atomos. Your ice caps will melt." Pulling the boat into the bank, Zagreus concluded with a smirk, "In the long run, these things tend to work themselves out, don't they?"

"I agree," responded Atomos half-heartedly, swinging his leg over the side of the boat and stepping into the moist grass. He glanced at the hill facing him. A stone staircase climbed up its side. Why would anyone bother laying so much stone at the bottom of the ocean? "Where's Azure?" he asked.

"Who?" Zagreus asked.

"My dragon. Where is she?" asked Atomos again.

"Oh! That's wonderful!" Venus jumped, giddy. "You've named her like an Atlantean."

"What do you mean?" questioned Atomos.

"As extensions of ourselves, all dragons bear the same first letter in their name as their rider. During the Warring Period, dragons and riders had to share their whole names. Luckily, that's not the case anymore. My dragon's name is Vulcan. He's the white one. Beautiful, isn't he? Zagreus named his dragon Zurvaan. He's the red dragon; you remember, right?"

"How could I forget such a terrifying creature?"

"Don't judge a book by its cover," corrected Zagreus forcefully.

"Sorry," Atomos said agreeably.

"We'll be able to see the dragon encampment soon enough," she reassured him. "Look, when we get to the top of the hill, you'll see."

They began trudging up the long stone staircase. Two columns connected by a half-circle stood at the top, making an archway. As they ascended, Venus set into her tirade. "Zagreus, how could you say that earlier? The knights have given us so much. Without them, we'd still be in the Warring Period. Everyone would be tearing each other's eyes out."

Like they aren't already, thought Atomos.

"Okay, sister, let's get the facts straight," countered Zagreus resentfully. "The library wasn't founded until the Cult Period. That was hundreds of years after when you're talking about. Before that, the Knights of Levi didn't have any power or influence in the Gyre. Do you understand those concepts?" he asked mockingly. "Before? After?"

"Stop it, Zagreus," shrieked Venus. "We're walking up the temple stairs! Don't you have any shame?" Her knuckles clenched white. Atomos wondered what had happened to their gloves.

"Not really." Zagreus shrugged, taking double steps. Eventually, he was so far out in front of them that he was almost halfway gone.

"So, how does this work?" inquired Atomos.

"I'll be your sponsor," whispered Venus, unusually quiet.

"My what?" asked Atomos.

"Your sponsor," she repeated. "First, you'll be blindfolded. Then, you'll receive the gift of life. Trust me, Atomos. You'll want to be blessed if you want to survive on the Isle of Immortals long."

"Why blindfolded?"

"After the fallout of the Warring Period, it became necessary to create the rules of a game that would both decide a champion to rule over the remaining rings and stand the test of time. Removing himself from the competition and declaring his own foresight over the matter, a daring madman among them plucked out his own eye with a branch he'd broken off a tree."

"All for a game?" gasped Atomos.

"All for the fountain."

"How's a blessing and some fountain water going to—"

"The games," she interjected, "are very important to us Atlanteans. We call them Kthulu, but you can't even begin to imagine the significance of this word. Kthulu is everything. Granted, it's not always like that. During the interval periods between the games, we mostly spend our days reflecting and planting dragon palms." She gestured to the trees. "But also, sometimes, we fly. Even your dragon can fly." Atomos hated pity even more than he enjoyed hearing about Azure. "She'll need help getting more than a few meters high, I'd say. The beginning of the games might be difficult. After that, though, everything should come naturally. Smooth sailing, probably!"

"Wouldn't count on it." Zagreus had stopped further up and was listening in. He kicked a corner piece of the stone steps and watched the rocks tumble down the hill. "After the fall of our city," he continued, matching their pace, "dragons were hunted to extinction. I don't blame the ancients for doing what they had to do. Since then, selective breeding has allowed them to regain all sorts of abilities."

"Does that mean dragons can breathe fire?" asked Atomos.

"Unfortunately not. That trait's been lost to time," grunted Zagreus.

"The winner is the first to find the golden ring and return it to the fountain," said Venus. "From then on, the new champion holds on to it and does with it whatever she wants, until the next games, of course, in twenty-five years."

"Twenty-five! That's almost twice how old I am. When you said 'long intervals,' I didn't think you meant—"

"A small price to pay to live in paradise," she retorted.

"Paradise found," muttered Atomos sarcastically.

"Might as well not even try. I mean, you don't seriously think you can win, do you?" asked Zagreus.

"What do you mean? Not everyone plays the Kthulu?"

"No, some don't," replied Venus. "But who cares about them? They won't be around long." Zagreus neared the top of the stairs. "Now, please, put this on, and don't say anything." Venus pulled a thin, black silk garment from under her gold Atlantean armor. Atomos wondered if she'd been using this cloth as a waistband. Venus wrapped the band around his nose and eyes. To his delight, it smelled incredibly floral.

"But, Venus, I was supposed to see Azure," Atomos remembered.

"Don't worry, you will," reassured the guardian. Between the corner of his right eye and his nose, Atomos made out a single triangle of light from which he could still see. When he got to the top of the stairs, he spied through his peephole a towering fountain standing at the center of a flat stone courtyard. Unlike the spout he'd seen in the ruins of the Atlantean temple, this elegant, cascading centerpiece was five levels high. Each level was marked by a beautifully inscribed bowl, but the words were all written in that same unintelligible script. The perimeter of the courtyard housed five other arches, each matching the one he had just passed through.

Venus led Atomos forward, directing his every step. From what little Atomos could see, other than Zagreus, Venus, and himself, six more Atlanteans had gathered in the courtyard. Three bowed down to the fountain on all fours, lowering their heads and tucking it between their hands and their knees. The other three stood there idly; however, from their squared shoulders and upright body language, Atomos felt all three of them eyeing him intently. The one in the back seemed so round and large that surely he could be an elephant. Besides him, however, Zagreus was the tallest.

Atomos stumbled over a small irregularity in the stones. Venus let go, and he fell to the ground. An audible gasp came from all those watching. That was close. He'd almost rolled an ankle. Atomos remembered to keep quiet during the fall; however, afterward, he raised his hands toward Venus, and all who were watching could immediately tell that Atomos was not blinded by the cover.

"He can see," shrieked a high-pitched voice. Atomos tore off his blindfold. The bright scenery subdued him. All stared in bewilderment. The three that had been bowing before even turned to watch. Oddly enough, in addition to their dark eyes and long ears, each of them seemed very similar in complexion. Behind the fountain, on the far end of the courtyard, another man, bald and wrinkled in a black-and-silver robe, dropped his cup from the excitement. Unlike the others, however, his robe was accented with gold. Despite his shocked expression, the bald man seemed torn between Atomos and the cup at his feet. Oddly, his round head, fit his long, sharp, black beard. As the man knelt, Atomos could just barely see, upon the man's old, wrinkly finger, a small, shiny ring of gold.

7

THE KNIGHT'S PRAYER

"Welcome to the Isle of Immortals, young human," uttered a low, comforting voice. Atomos felt a hand on his shoulder. The older bald man who'd dropped his cup leaned over him. "I am Agathon, leader of the Knights of Levi and oldest living Atlantean. Tell me, who are you? Be honest. No matter what you tell me, young human, I will come to know the truth."

This seemed unlikely. Agathon didn't seem that old. There were only a few silver streaks in his black beard, nothing very impressive. Even Pueo had more gray. Still, Atomos definitely noticed a few dark spots on his long Atlantean ears. How could this guy possibly be the oldest living Atlantean? Was everyone dying? What about the dragons? Did they die too? Perhaps, under the right conditions, they were immortal, like polyps on a coral or, perhaps, jellyfish.

Eventually, Atomos replied, "I am Atomos."

"Hello, Atomos. The Isle of Immortals welcomes you. Now, what is it that you want? Humans always want something."

"I want to be blessed."

"Well then, fantastic. Today, we have a new member," shouted Agathon, loud enough for the whole courtyard to hear. He helped Atomos to his feet, grinning out the side of his mouth. "Actually, you just so happen to be joining us on a very special day. In addition to our daily worship of the Leviathan, on this day, two days before the start of Kthulu, we also celebrate our separation from the forgotten creator. On this day of terrestrial remembrance, we pray our sacrifice was not in vain." These words reminded Atomos of Haloa, the first Hawaiian, and the unforgettable lesson that had always stuck with him: be kind to the earth.

Everyone gathered around and joined hands. "Since ancient Rome, no human has been one of us. Now, today, we begin anew."

Atomos glanced to the side, privately agitated to learn that he was not the first human ever to enter the Gyre.

"But, s-sir," intruded one of the Atlanteans who'd been crouching on the ground. "He, he b-broke the pact. He's, he's seen the f-fountain before drinking from the c-c-cup." The skinny Atlantean who spoke had no hair anywhere on his body. His head was lumpy and misshapen. He wore a black-and-silver robe like Agathon and the other knights standing in the back. However, unlike the others, he spoke as if Atomos wasn't right there in front of him, which, in addition to his mannerisms, proved extremely annoying.

"It's rather obvious, isn't it?" Agathon shot a glance straight at Atomos. The large, dark bags under his eyes were extremely hard to ignore. He, like all the knights, wore a wooden, magenta rosary. "The Leviathan has blessed him. Tell me then, my human child, which stream did you drink from before arriving here?"

"Drink?" asked Atomos, puzzled. He hadn't drunk anything.

"Why didn't you tell us?" shouted Venus, overjoyed.

"I—" started Atomos, stunned.

"We drink from the fountain to heal ourselves," interjected Venus, very enthused. "This is why we live down here. The Gyre is a holy place."

Atomos was downright perplexed. This Leviathan creature must be some sort of Atlantean god or something. Better to keep quiet so as to avoid sounding overly offensive. "But, seriously, if you've been blessed, Atomos, then that means the L—"

"I didn't drink anything," interjected Atomos.

"Don't lie in my presence!" erupted Agathon. "I will not tolerate deception. Now, I understand it is just ceremonial at this point for you, but still, I would be honored if you would join us, Atomos. Each day, we begin with morning prayer at six, and then each day at nine, the evening prayer." Agathon confidently scanned the courtyard as he spoke. Everyone seemed in agreement.

"What do I pray for?" asked Atomos. "For Atlantis?"

"For three thousand years, we have remembered our city's drowning as the loss of our earthly identity. The greatest aspects of our culture, gone forever. Most importantly, our relationship with the earth has not changed, unlike with the sun. In our prayers, and in everything we do, we combat this solar solitude with solidarity and tradition, which, of course, extends the spiritual realm to the possession of the public. As such, we are communal beyond death."

Everyone nodded. *Isn't tradition just thinly veiled peer pressure from dead people?* Atomos wondered sardonically. Agathon grinned and gestured to the fountain. "Now, if everyone will join hands." Venus and Zagreus grabbed hold of him on his left and right. Across the fountain, beside Agathon, Atomos saw the elephant-sized knight grab hold of the knight next to him and roll his eyes. "Leviathan, in addition to your divine will, allow us to join in your wisdom."

What was going on? What was this vortex business? *Am I in some sort of strange, phenomenal dream?* Atomos let go of Venus and raised his hand.

"Excuse me," he muttered, clearing his throat. Everyone opened their eyes and stared at him, baffled. Nobody moved a muscle. Was he not supposed to do that or something? Instantly, Atomos was filled with regret. Nevertheless, he continued, "I'm sorry, but who is the Leviathan?"

"Atomos," responded Agathon, unfazed by the question, "I admit, prayer is one of the most powerful tools in my spiritual work. However, even I cannot change your mind. Only you can do that. As the leader of the Knights of Levi, my responsibility is solely to interpret the Leviathan's intent. I do not wish to convert you. But, in my humble opinion, your question is better stated not 'Who is the Leviathan' but rather 'What is the Leviathan?'"

"What is it, then?" asked Atomos. Everyone remained silent.

"The Leviathan is not something to take lightly, Atomos. It's very real, trust me. We've no way of knowing its size for certain. But that's because, from inside the Gyre, we can only ever see a small part of its shadow at any one time; that's by design, of course. A fraction is all we're meant to see."

"How do you talk to it?" asked Atomos, confused.

"I know this might be hard to imagine, human. Expand your mind for a moment, if you can. Try to think of the Gyre as an energy grid. The community's collective prayers travel from the fountain, along natural electromagnetic lines, out to the Leviathan. Our intense emotions and thoughts of love, peace, and harmony are all felt and reciprocated; this is communication." Agathon smiled at Atomos, but the boy still didn't understand. "Thoughts are energy, Atomos, like lights and shadows. All things are manifested in thought. The ancients believed thoughts and prayers traveled around the earth like beams. They were right, of course. They developed teleportation."

"Oh, okay, I understand," said Atomos, lying.

"All right, good. Well, then, Atomos, if I may, can we resume?"

Atomos nodded, slightly embarrassed. He rejoined hands with Venus and Zagreus. Everyone closed their eyes.

"Good. Now, decide in advance the emotion you wish to send out. Remember, the vortex must know your heart's true desire. Once you have that, visualize a beam of light coming from the highest point in the Gyre, straight down into the center of the fountain. Now, place the whole of your mind's intent into this light. Visualize yourself at the center, healing. Project your loved ones if you wish to heal them. When you have finished, give thanks to the Leviathan. The Knight's Prayer is complete."

Atomos felt an intense weight pushing down on his forehead. What had his intention been? He couldn't remember. There was only a blank gap in his memory where the thought had been. *Perhaps*, Atomos considered, *I never really had much of an intention at all.*

"Great. All of you may now partake." Suddenly, Agathon let go of the others and walked around the fountain, over to Atomos.

"Don't mind if I do," grunted the elephant man, grabbing the cup.

"You don't need to drink from the fountain," whispered Agathon to Atomos. "You've already been blessed. Actually, I have something else for you." The others began talking among themselves, surrounding the enormous knight. "The rings of Atlantis have magical properties, which possess supernatural abilities. Since the first of the scholars, the golden rings have remained under the protection of the Knights of Levi. The green rings, on the other hand, belong to the guardians. Apart from the day of the games, during the ceremony, none have ever held the ring but the honored champion; never, that is, until today."

Atomos stared deep into Agathon's intense black eyes.

"If not you, who else?" As he removed the gold ring from his finger, Agathon placed it in his palm and extended his hand, offering it to Atomos and whispering reassuringly, "This is more than a gift. This is your destiny. You are the modern Achilles." Atomos felt everyone's eyes on them. "Now, go on. Take it."

Atomos was hesitant, inspecting Agathon's crooked smile. Atomos took the ring, although he decided not to put it on. Agathon immediately turned around. "For the Isle of Immortals!" The theologian raised his arms and all cheered.

"That's amazing, Atomos," yelled Venus.

"Everyone, listen!" roared Agathon. "My vision has led me to realize what our true purpose shall be. According to the Leviathan, I must leave now, but I will be back soon. Come with me, Venus. It was you who brought Atomos to us, and so you too shall share in the reward of a lifetime. The Leviathan has spoken." Agathon extended his arm toward the teenage girl, who was surprised to hear her name. "We haven't much time," he persisted. "We must go quickly."

Agathon and Venus left together, hand in hand. They started down one of the six sets of stairs, away from the courtyard. Before reaching the bottom of the hill, the pair took a sharp turn along a cobblestone path on top of the mountainside. Atomos didn't care, but Zagreus was furious. The thought of Agathon and his sister alone together was obviously quite repulsive. Still, he didn't say anything in front of the group. Zagreus stormed down the stairs, passing under the closest adjacent arch, back to his canoe. As he left, others arrived. The knights passed Agathon's cup around among the newcomers as more and more piled into the courtyard. None were knights or guardians, simply wearing their black robes. Atomos remained the only human. In a low, deep, rumbling voice, the large elephant man spoke:

"Drink, friends! Let the cup soothe your lips and quench your thirst. The elixir of life is for all. Even you, little legend." For the first time, Atomos noticed that the large man had only a single eye. "Where are my manners? I'm so lost. I've forgotten to introduce myself. I am Argus, knight and watchman. Haven't seen anything yet, though. I guess you could say it's a becoming post." Argus laughed at himself. While the others talked behind the giant, Atomos heard the hairless knight near the back spitting and stammering.

"It's a pleasure to meet you, Argus." Atomos extended his hand. As he did, however, he remembered he held the golden ring in his palm. What was the point of anything now? He could go home anytime he wanted. Really, he only needed one more thing. "Excuse me?"

"Yes?" replied the friendly cyclops.

"Where's the dragon encampment?"

Argus pointed toward the lake in the center of the island, between the mountains. "Follow the trail to the lake. There, you'll find your dragon." Before Atomos was able to ask the cyclops any more questions, an angry voice erupted from behind him.

"Hello, everyone. Forget about us?" Oberon and Titania, each of whom still wore their gold armor, joined them in the knights' courtyard on the mount. Neither wore their helmets, nor did they carry their helmets or signature tridents. "Have you all finished the Vortex Prayer already, or were we just not invited?" The hairless knight ran over to Oberon and his sister. Frantically, he bowed to the guardians. Then, leaning in very close, he whispered in Oberon's ear, "So, it's true."

Oberon approached Atomos furiously. The muscular Atlantean grabbed Atomos by the wrist. "After everything I've done for the Gyre, Agathon's just giving it away to a human. After everything we've done to protect it from them? The games are in two days! My family's been protecting the dragons from the surface world for thousands of years. My dragon's the most fearsome in the Gyre. I've seen yours, human. Pathetic. The thing's barely even hatched." Oberon turned to face everyone. "Osiris is better than any other dragon on this godforsaken rock." He spun back around and stared down at the gold ring Atomos had in his palm, envious. His own green ring shined on his finger. Suddenly, he smiled. "What was I thinking?" Oberon turned, looking up at Argus. "Tell me. Where are Agathon and the other guardians?"

"They've all gone," responded Argus. "I'm not too sure where." Oberon turned to Atomos, then back to the hairless knight, and then back to Atomos.

"Nereus? Send word to everyone on the island. In one hour, Atomos and I, Oberon, proud guardian of the Gyre, duel. Son of Triton versus the modern Achilles. What do you say? Winner keeps the ring." The boastful overconfidence in Oberon was too much for Atomos. Almost instinctively, since they'd first met, he'd despised the abrasive, rugged Atlantean. He wanted the satisfaction of taking him one-on-one.

"Why wait?" replied Atomos arrogantly.

Oberon turned and left the courtyard. Nereus followed closely behind this guardian. Oberon's sister, Titania, who until now had always been either too timid or too spiteful to speak, waited. She stared at Atomos coldly. For the first time, he saw the beauty in her deep, black eyes as she shook her head back and forth disapprovingly.

"You'll regret this," whispered Titania, so faint that Atomos almost missed hearing her entirely. Then, a fog formed back over her eyes.

She shook her head once more, turned, and walked down the stairs, following her brother. Palm trees of every shape, size, and sort garnished the mountainside on his short walk from the courtyard to the top of the volcano. After trekking through the jungle and hiking up the steep trail alone, he reached a point where he could see out over the trees. In the courtyard below, a great number of people had gathered around to watch him. Atomos wondered how they'd be able to see the action from so far. Reaching the summit, he felt the great heat of the lava rising out of the ground. He picked up a rock and tossed it in. It didn't skip. It caught on fire and sank. Being that they were at the bottom of the ocean, he'd half expected a geyser shooting water vapor into the air. Perhaps this was where the cycle ended. A great number of noises erupted from the jungle. Tall trees snapped and shattered. It was Oberon, arriving upon the back of his fearsome black dragon.

"You still got the ring?" grunted the Atlantean.

"What, did you think I'd lose it?" Atomos pulled it out of his pocket.

"Never mind," grunted Oberon. "Put it on the ground, under a rock. The winner will come back to claim it." Atomos did. "Good. I'll be over there, waiting."

As Oberon pointed, Atomos couldn't help but notice once more his two missing fingers. How'd he lose them when the Gyre was oozing with the elixir of life? Losing them on the surface seemed unlikely. Oberon and his dragon circled to the other side of the volcano. Behind them, Atomos was surprised to see Azure climbing the volcano. Zagreus was riding her. Also, the wound on her leg had completely healed.

"Zagreus?" yelled Atomos, happy to see the guardian. "What're you doing here? Why're you riding my dragon?"

"You've got a lot of nerve, Atomos," replied Zagreus. "When I heard about this duel, I wasn't even going to watch. The dragon encampment isn't looking after itself. My dragon doesn't care much, I'm sure." Atomos remembered all too well the red beast that had cornered him on the iceberg's ledge. "Not even an hour goes by and I hear there's no Kthulu this year. You're the champion."

"Oberon might have something to say about that."

"So, you and Oberon are the only ones who get to compete? Seems fair. I don't care one way or the other. Whatever happens, happens. Imagine my surprise, though, when I look over and I see her in a stall." He gestured to Azure. "An hour goes by, still no human in sight."

"I didn't know we were dueling dragons."

Zagreus dismounted Azure, turned, and walked back down into the jungle, silent and completely nonchalant.

"Thank you," yelled Atomos.

Zagreus didn't even look back. Noticing a flower at his feet, Atomos grabbed hold of the small blue spikes that protruded from Azure's back and swung himself into position. There was no feeling in the world that compared to riding on a dragon's back, on land or in water. Azure took him to the top of the volcano where Oberon was waiting.

"Now, Achilles, let's see what you're worth," yelled Oberon from across the boiling lake of lava. His black dragon extended its sixty-foot wings out to each side. Azure did the same. Atomos felt the extreme heat on his face. As the hot air caught in her wings, globs of sweat trickled down his forehead, dripping onto Azure's back. Both Atomos and Oberon began to rise a few inches into the air while their dragons' hind legs and tails remained planted.

Before Azure had gotten more than six feet off the ground, though, Atomos slipped and fell, tumbling off her back, unable to catch himself. By this point, Azure'd been almost upright. There was nothing she could do. Dropping more than thirty feet, Atomos landed, quite abrasively, in the branches of a palm tree. Never before had he fallen like this. Never.

ALONE IN THE JUNGLE

After picking himself up and brushing off, Atomos walked through the trees, back to the courtyard, alone and ashamed. What was he going to do now? No ring. No Azure. That didn't matter anymore anyway. Even if he got her back, he wouldn't know how to ride her. He wouldn't be able to beat all these experienced dragon riders, especially when the games were happening in a mere two days. Kthulu was all about flying. Another twenty-five years of training and he still might not be ready.

Atomos had never felt more stupid than he did at this moment. Oberon had the ring. He was the champion. It was all over. That was it. He'd failed. Usually, when he said he'd do something, he did it. What was he without his word? Atomos was ashamed. It took nearly half an hour for Atomos to walk back. Would everyone treat him differently now? Hopefully, it wouldn't be embarrassing. Atomos reached the top step. He walked through the archway. The Knights of Levi all stood and stared at him. The decorative, layered fountain had stopped flowing. In the cobblestone courtyard, standing among the engraved fountain and the other five archways, nearly everyone was there—everyone except Zagreus.

"What are you doing back here?" yelled the knight opposite Argus whose name Atomos didn't know. Atomos also didn't know how to respond. Neither, it seemed, did the rest of the Atlanteans. Nobody said anything. Upon seeing Atomos return to the courtyard, however, a large smile stretched across Agathon's wrinkled old face. Quickly, the grin disappeared.

"Back so soon, are we, Atomos? You've lost my ring, haven't you?"

"Oberon has it now," whimpered Atomos, nervous.

"Oh, I see. Well then, I suppose I was wrong. I misjudged you, human. Even with your divine gift, you're only human. You couldn't protect that ring. You're not smart enough. You're not at all who I thought you'd be."

"I fell. How can I fight when I can't stand?" pleaded Atomos, desperate, almost belligerent.

Agathon responded with a stern lecture. "You should learn to control your temper, Atomos. Your strength may have gotten you this far, but clearly it was dumb luck. I mean, seriously, if anything, it sounds to me like you lost the ring to Oberon in a battle of wits."

Nereus let out a loud, cackling laugh. Venus gave a sinister smile.

"If only you were a true modern Achilles," joked Agathon. "Perhaps if you trained in his arena, you might pick up a thing or two. Watch your ankle, though. Wouldn't want you to slip." Agathon snickered. He patted the back of the mysterious unnamed knight, who let out a cold, confident grin. Like the others, he too seemed only a few years older than Atomos. Long, thin black hair hung low over his eyes. He was irritatingly handsome.

"Can't you hear? Get lost," yelled the confident knight.

Who was this vicious character? Atomos had nothing to say. He turned and headed back down the steps. Everyone started talking behind him. Atomos didn't care. He didn't need those people. He was used to being alone. He'd learn to fly himself. Atomos walked through the sand by the little lake. He thought of Azure. She'd probably flown back to the dragon encampment. *Just follow the path; that's what Argus said.* Once he got Azure back, he'd take her to the Achilles arena and learn everything he could about dragon dueling. Then, right before the games, he and Azure would find Oberon, steal his golden ring, and return to the surface. Nobody would ever see either of them again.

Atomos peered ahead, down the bank toward the dragon encampment. Never had he felt so alone—or, at least, not that he could remember. He couldn't let anything like that ever happen again. Atomos desperately needed to prove himself. But not everything is what it seems, especially not here. Why should he be shadowboxing Achilles? As he walked, Zagreus appeared through the trees.

"Zagreus?"

"What do you want?"

"Venus told me Azure—"

"Atomos," replied Zagreus at once. "I can't take you to the encampment to get your dragon. The council doesn't allow any Atlantean to enter the encampment, not even the knights. Only we guardians are allowed in."

"Why?" questioned Atomos. "Isn't that unfair?"

"When we're not searching for lost dragons, we're looking after them. Fair isn't part of it. We all do our part. If there's a challenge, the challengers can also go in and claim their dragon, as you found out—or, rather, didn't find out."

"But that's why I need your help."

"Nope, that's it. That's as far as we go."

"But—"

"No." Zagreus was already well gone around the corner. Now all that Atomos could think to do was set out to find the Achilles arena. Twists and turns filled the trail, trekking through the jungle, but the terrain wasn't all too difficult, despite his feet being bare and his legs being so short and stout. At the end of an hour, however, Atomos was thoroughly worn down and most definitely too tired to walk. No longer was he carelessly bounding over branches like in the beginning. Mud caked the insides of his legs. The air was hot and sticky. Water droplets formed beads under his wavy, ginger hairline. Atomos wiped his brow. The humidity of the Gyre had never seemed so thick before. Sweat rolled down his temple, neck, and back. It tasted quite salty.

Luckily, Atomos noticed, there hadn't been any bugs. Now that he thought of it, he hadn't seen a single bug, not once, the whole time he'd been here. No birds, no bugs, nothing at all. No fruit hung off the trees, nor did Atomos see any flowers around, dead, blooming, or otherwise. How were there no flowers besides on the volcano? Atomos dearly missed the coconuts and bananas that grew on the trees back home. He didn't feel that hungry. He mostly missed the way they tasted. *Wait. Why don't I feel hungry?* Since the moment he'd met these Atlanteans, nobody'd mentioned eating. The Knights of Levi wouldn't have a feast anytime soon, he realized, thinking back to home.

Atomos trudged on through the thick, green rainforest, pushing past countless bushes in his path. The scraping and shuffling sounded like little squeaks in the silence. Although these Atlanteans claimed to be immortal and all righteous, they were simply people. They were no more alive than humans. Just because most of humanity had chosen to forget their past didn't mean they didn't want peace. Considering how many of them focused on their private lives, first and foremost, inner peace seemed like it should be their first priority. The last humans to come to the Gyre were Romans; they clearly had no outer peace. Why were they more moral? What about their rituals and human sacrifices? How barbaric. *Are these practices justified by their emotional range? Is this process necessary for a person to overcome their trauma? Do they have a need to rejoin the group?* Atomos thought of *Frankenstein*, the clever outsider and his secret experiment.

The path opened up into a stream with an adjacent grassy bank. Atomos took a pebble he'd picked up off a fallen stump and threw it into the running water.

"I have rituals." Atomos shrugged, thinking back to all the times Pueo had sat around the fire and prayed over their food. Although, perhaps this was more of a habit. But at the same time, most places were so inward and individualistic. Nobody left their house, not in the Age of Aquarius. Even sports suffered. *Although, as Pueo would say, sports used to be all about ritual. Maybe I could ask—*

Atomos stopped in his muddy tracks. He was surprised he'd let that slip. Had he forgotten Pueo was gone? He didn't need anyone to take care of him.

Past the grassy bank he'd been following, inside the winding stream and tied to one of the big boulders, Atomos saw a small canoe. As he drew nearer, bounding through the cold water, Atomos recognized the vessel as the same he'd rode in on. This canoe belonged to Venus and Zagreus. Atomos scanned left and right. He surveyed the trees, the grass, the bushes, and the boulders. Neither of the siblings were in sight. *Well,* thought Atomos, *surely they won't mind if I take their canoe. After all, they are guardians. They can access the dragon encampment whenever they want.*

He pulled a paddle from underneath the canoe's seats. An hour later, he passed under a large archway beside a brick wall. Another fifteen minutes went by before, suddenly, Atomos heard a deafeningly loud, nervous shriek. The sound seemed to be coming from downstream.

"Help me! Help me!" it cried. A tall, skinny boy ran from the grassy bank and into the river until submerged up to his chest, stopping about five yards away. "I've lost my pet. Please, help me find him," he pleaded. After Atomos stopped the boat, the skinny Atlantean looked downstream and cupped his hands over his mouth, drawing attention to his pointy nose and buck teeth. "Ponos?"

His hair was silver, a little like Venus and Zagreus, although his was a great deal shorter than either of theirs. "Ponos? Where are you?"

"Pono?" Atomos whispered to himself. That was a Hawaiian word. There was no English translation. If there were one, though, it'd probably be closest to "righteous." The Hawaiian state motto, *Ua Mau ke Ea o ka Āina i ka Pono,* meant "the life of the land is maintained by the righteous." But still, the word *righteous* didn't do justice to the word's true meaning. The level of balance and harmony meant by Hawaiians when they said "pono" was unmatched.

"I've lost my pet! You've got to help me! Please?"

"Get in," asserted Atomos. "We don't have any time to lose."

"Thank you." The Atlantean swung his leg over the side of the canoe. He was about the same age as Atomos, maybe a year older, but much skinnier. Rocking the boat more than needed, he climbed in, splashing water everywhere. Algae and mud covered his clothes. The swamp water was murkier than elsewhere on the island, Atomos noticed. The boy's black robes had gold trimming, like the other knights, albeit torn and tattered.

"What's your name?" From the look in his eye, Atomos could tell the knight wanted him to scan the water's surface more actively.

"Apollodorus."

"I'm Atomos. What did you say your pet looked like, Apollo—?"

"He's a frog. Slimy, green, you know?"

"So, did the knights send you here?" asked Atomos.

"No way," responded Apollodorus. "Why would the knights care about me?"

The Atlantean was obviously lying.

"Did you say your pet frog's name was Pono?" asked Atomos.

"How did you say it?" countered Apollodorus.

"In my culture, to my people, the word *pono* means being in a state of harmony. Finding one's pono is to find balance with oneself."

"You said your name was Atomos?" replied the boy, slightly hesitant. Atomos nodded in affirmation. "Old Democritus, interesting." Apollodorus nodded as if working the pieces like a puzzle in his mind. "Well, no, Atomos, sadly, my pet's name is not Pono. It's Ponos, with an *s* at the end. Ponos is the personification of hardship in Greek. Quite literally, he's an expression of my hard work back at the library. According to the *Theogony*, Ponos was the son of the goddess Eris, the daughter of Nyx, the night. Haven't you heard of the epic poem *The Shield of Heracles*?"

"No, but that's rad," countered Atomos. "I was almost named Herc—"

"Not Hercules, Heracles," interrupted Apollodorus rudely. "They're different people, you know. Although, it's very human of you to make that mistake. Did you think Poseidon wanted you humans to name that planet Neptune in 1846? The Greeks and the Romans were different civilizations, hundreds of years apart. There's a whole sea of differences between them and their respective cultures."

Atomos was offended by the librarian's rude behavior. *I have never met someone so eager to correct anyone and everyone. It has to be the most annoying—*

"There! I see him. I'm coming, Ponos!"

The green frog was very large, maybe the size of a grapefruit. It perched on a lily pad. Tiny ripples formed all around. Apollodorus jumped out, creating a huge splash that not only rocked Atomos but also knocked the frog off the lily pad, into the water. Apollodorus desperately grabbed for the leaping amphibian, but, expectedly, it hopped onto the bank and got away. Atomos couldn't take his eyes off the librarian. He was too amused.

Apollodorus chased the frog onto the bank, but alas, the slimy creature slipped through his hands once more before jumping away into the green grass. The deep grass obscured his landing from view. Every time Apollodorus fell only to then get back up, however, he'd run another five feet in another direction, jump, and then fall again. Finally, the librarian emerged, grasping the amphibian firmly, lifting it like a trophy above his head.

"Victory!" he yelled. Atomos hooted and hollered, even louder and more excited than the time Pueo had risen with that fish on his spear.

"Come on back, Hera-clueless," yelled Atomos. He liked being with Apollodorus more than he liked being alone. "To the library then?"

"Thank you," said Apollodorus. "That would be very nice, indeed." He sat in the front of the canoe. Ponos croaked in anger, jumping around the hull.

At last, when they'd reached the long, mossy, stone bridge, Atomos knew they'd arrived. It was hard to miss. He looked up. At the top of the library, Atomos saw a golden light emanating from the tallest tower. He furrowed his brow. Could this be the location of the ring?

9

THE HEIR OF POSEIDON

Atomos docked the canoe off to the side of the river, wedging it on the grassy bank by the library. Before he'd finished pulling the boat halfway out of the water, Apollodorus stepped out and started toward the structure. Displaying no intention to turn or say anything at all, much less to give thanks for the ride, Apollodorus continued on. Atomos was unimpressed. All this after having helped him find his frog, given him a lift back, and tolerated his obnoxious information dumps. Did he assume everyone had the same information he had, being a hermit? Atomos should've left him behind.

"Apollodorus! Wait!" Atomos stood in the canoe. "What kind of research are you working on?" His eyes drifted again to the tower. The architecture nearest the library's tallest tower displayed mermaid gargoyles. Perhaps there was no golden ring, but at least the librarian would have some knowledge about Achilles. Atomos would need to know what happened to the ancient human warrior here in the Gyre if he was going to prevent his own demise. *History's like nature,* thought Atomos. *She repeats herself. Maybe she doesn't like to, but she does, ultimately. The more that changes, the more stays the same.*

"I can show you if you'd like," answered Apollodorus, offering to guide the way with his hand. After less than half a second, though, he pulled his hand back toward his face, biting his fingernails. Apollodorus had never had a visitor before. For the first time in a long time, he genuinely felt excited.

Croak!

The librarian tucked his hands into his robe, pinning down his little experiment, careful not to let the devilish creature slip loose once more. In defiance, Ponos let out a series of deep, bellowing croaks.

Apollodorus led Atomos across the old stone bridge. All of the pillars were covered in bright-green moss. Perhaps this library had been here from the beginning, or at least as long as the courtyard. Atomos wondered how this, too, could've made it to the bottom of the ocean.

Standing on top of the bridge, Atomos saw the valley below and a glorious waterfall. The beautiful scenery did nothing to cure his fervent thoughts. Where was he? What was the reason for him being on this island? How would he get home? Stepping off the bridge and onto the library's outer wall, part of his foot had landed on an unfortunately placed gap in the stones. Landing awkwardly, Atomos fell down. Only a thin margin prevented him from a terrible fate, his leg having fallen through, left dangling above another gushing waterfall. What a dangerous place to stumble. Perhaps the gap was for water runoff, drainage, or some type of irrigation. With such an abundance of water all around, Atomos was unsure why the Atlanteans would need to have an aqueduct. Did it ever even rain?

Walking a half pace in front of Atomos, the librarian happily showed off his collection of dusty trinkets and half-torn scrolls, describing each in unnecessary detail.

"Most of the library was destroyed long ago. These scrolls have seen a lot." The skinny Atlantean held one up to the light. There was no ceiling. The walls were tall and covered in moss. The bookshelves—or rather, scroll-shelves—cast long, looming shadows. "The greatest significance of these writings, however, is their survival, alongside the knights, who hid in the crystal caves, avoiding the bloodshed of the late Warring Period."

"What's this one about?" Atomos picked up the scroll closest to himself and handed it to Apollodorus. All were lined up and spread out inside the minimalist, wooden bookshelves. In total, Atomos counted maybe forty scrolls.

"This is a prophecy the guardians brought in two centuries ago."[3]

"Who wrote it?"

"An Irish poet, W. B. Yeats. He wrote fairy tales. You're not going to make me read poetry, will you? Here, read this one." He handed Atomos a scroll. "It's called *The Decline and Fall of Indigo*. I don't understand why humans think their laws are so powerful. Why have trust? Empires are built from trade and protection, but never actually deliver what they promise."

"That's it?" Atomos was disappointed. "I don't care about the history of other humans. I'm a loner." He went back to studying the astounding detail on the wall, running his fingers along its chipped edges, adorned with more of the same lavish script. How did the Atlanteans know so much about humans when so much of their own history was lost? *Why speak the language of a culture you despise?* Atomos didn't understand. Moments later, Apollodorus ran up to him again with even more scrolls.

"Here's the story of the founders, *Prometheus & Pandora*. Yeah, that's probably the first thing you ought to know. Although, everything in it happened more than three thousand years ago," admitted Apollodorus.

"What else do you have?" asked Atomos.

"Perhaps, instead, we could read . . ." Apollodorus pulled out two more scrolls. "Yes, here we have *Tactics of Kthulu* and *Dragon Breeds & Anatomy*. Didn't you mention that you might need a bit of help learning how to fly?"

Atomos took both of the scrolls and then turned to the side, rather embarrassed. "Anything else?"

---

3   *The Second Coming* (1919)

"Yes," continued Apollodorus. "Over here, we have the original copy of the first Oceanic Contract from the days before the knights' reformations ended the Warring Period. Over here, there's *The Epic of King Triton*, the tale of the first Atlantean to ever be banished from the Isle of Immortals." Apollodorus's face grew somber and his lip quivered.

"What's going on?" questioned Atomos.

"I just . . ." The librarian looked as if he were going to burst into tears.

"It's all good, mate." Atomos put his hand on the librarian's skinny left shoulder. "We don't have to go there. Take your mind off it. Why don't you tell me more about that ancient king?"

"During the early days of Kthulu, the strategy was very simple: get to the gold ring first and you win," grumbled Apollodorus, still unhappy. His hunch had worsened.

"Isn't that how it works now?"

Apollodorus eyed Atomos, suspicious of a joke. Realizing the human was serious, however, the librarian appeared lively again. "Aren't you glad I gave you those scrolls? Obviously, there isn't only one strategy," he laughed. "How would it work every time? Still, a simple plan will be of much use to you. Remember, the games consist of five Kthulu tactics based on the five disbanded cults: Triton, Bastet, Raijin, and the married duo, Typhon and Echidna."

"Why should I care? If they're gone, they're gone," concluded Atomos.

"There's a reason each of them grew so famous," responded the skinny Atlantean. "Only the ancient kings and the island's founders are more highly regarded in our history. Open it. You'll understand." Atomos opened his scroll, reading five lines of script:

The Five Histories of Kthulu: Year 1775
In the sky, the dangerous dragon has the biggest horns.
In the water, the fastest dragon has the strongest tail.
Up the mountains, the dragon with talons climbs.
In the caves, the brightest dragon hides.
In flight, the quick dragon survives.

"That first tactic has always been defensive by nature," added Apollodorus, disturbing Atomos as he read. "And notice the difference in word choice between 'In the sky' and 'In flight'?"

"Seventeen seventy-five?" exclaimed Atomos. "This scroll is almost five hundred years old!" Atomos was amazed by how well the parchment was preserved. It was dusty, but there were no tears or holes.

"Actually," replied Apollodorus, "Atlanteans count their years from the fall of their civilization onward. That's closer to about five hundred years before humans celebrate the birth of their king. So, in your people's time, it must have been written in about the year 1275?"

"Wow! Nearly a thousand years," exclaimed Atomos. "How do you know so much about us? Is it all from books and poems?"

"For the most part, yes, that's it. The guardians have been keeping our watch over humanity." Apollodorus shrugged.

"What do you mean?"

"Well, actually, under humanity," he said, correcting himself. "Every so often, there will be a human that discovers our secrets. Before they can publish their findings, however, the guardians find them and destroy any and all evidence they've collected. You have no idea how many scrolls in this library are covered in blood."

Croak!

"Somehow or another," he continued, "word still got out about our island, albeit under a whole host of names: Eden, Avalon, Valhalla, you name it. Once word got out about our 'fountain of youth,' though, everything went completely mad. Some self-proclaimed king of comedy mislabeled the Atlanteans the 'Assassins of the Tyre,' or then again, was it the prince? It doesn't matter. Anyway, eventually, we got to him."

"What does all this mean?" questioned Atomos.

"In nearly every case," answered the librarian, "the humans foretell of a day of reckoning, eons in the future, when all of humanity surpasses death. Also, in every case, the creator separates the 'worthy' from the 'unworthy' before rescuing his chosen few from the chaos. Being from the Gyre, though, we Atlanteans know a future of this kind is categorically impossible. Humanity is simply too large to save. Unfortunately, however, this has also become our problem. Despite the guardians' best efforts, their legends persist. Some suspect a spy. How else could they have known about the octopus's garden beneath the waves?"

"What?" questioned Atomos. "I thought it was a giant squid that protected the portal, not an oversized octopus."

"That's not what they said!" Apollodorus was livid. "Doesn't matter. They're both cephalopods. They walk on their heads."

"What does any of this have to do with Kthulu?" asked Atomos impatiently. He couldn't believe how incredibly long-winded the librarian could be. Couldn't Apollodorus tell what he was after?

"Nothing, now that you mention it," replied Apollodorus.

"C'mon, library guy," nudged Atomos, "why don't you tell me—"

"Actually," interrupted Apollodorus, characteristically rude, "you're right. Triton did have something to do with Kthulu. He cheated. He attacked another Atlantean in the water before the last call of Kthulu, before the start of the games." Atomos was puzzled. "Triton was first to reach the golden ring, but even before pleading to the council, his rivals had already organized against him. He was banished. From that day onward, Kthulu tactics were born and the First Cult was forged in his name, making him a king."

"You're telling me that there were five banished Atlantean kings?"

"And queens," interjected Apollodorus. "Two of them were queens."

"Well, there aren't kings and queens anymore. So, what? They all got sucked out into the vacuum of the deep, into absolute darkness, utter nothingness, all to get eaten by the Leviathan?"

"First of all, Atomos," began Apollodorus, "the ocean isn't a vacuum. The Isle of Immortals is in the deep, which means that we're at least a thousand fathoms below sea level. But also, we may be up to twenty times that deep. Who knows? The ocean's a vast body of water and stretches from tropical waters to frigid polar regions, from shallow seabeds to the deepest ocean trenches. We could be anywhere. Maybe we're not even in the Pacific. Maybe we're near India. The point is we are, distinctly, not nowhere," Apollodorus took a deep breath. "Secondly, not everyone who's banished is thrown out. Some more fortunate souls are simply told not to participate. Either way, to be banished in the way you're describing, one must've broken the Oceanic Contract—no person shall attempt to kill or fatally wound another. Still, strangely enough, nobody remembers the name of who King Triton killed."

Croak!

"So, Oberon and Titania are descendants of Triton?"

"Yes," replied Apollodorus.

"I don't understand. Who was he?"

"At his trial, he claimed to be the heir of Poseidon, the last great king of Atlantis. Of course, Poseidon wasn't the only great king. There was Neptune, Pontus, Nereus, and Thalassar," listed Apollodorus. "All of them were descendants of a line of kings going back to Oceanus, all Telchines. Not the Nereus you know, though, Atomos," noted the librarian.

"So, Oberon's a king?" remarked Atomos.

"No, not exactly. He's more like a prince," replied Apollodorus. "When the Knights of Levi disbanded the cults, they also revoked our birthrights."

"Everyone?" asked Atomos.

"Which reminds me," continued Apollodorus. He held up three fingers. "Lastly, contrary to what you might have heard, there isn't a bigger fish out there, just a shadow. The Leviathan isn't real. Some people would run over and cover my mouth for saying such a thing." This was a reaction unfamiliar to Atomos. Back home on the island, Pueo had always let him speak his mind. But who was he to have a voice here? After all, to him, the Leviathan wasn't anything special. To him, even if it was real, it was probably just another terrifying giant squid.

Apollodorus continued, "Legends tell of a creature so big that the act of defeating it would itself be an illusion. Despite its immensity and godlike presence, the knights wrote that the Leviathan must have been blessed by our creator. To have sustained such life in a barren wasteland is itself a miracle. Therefore, they theorized it must be the creature's divine intention to keep our company." Apollodorus slowed these last three words. Was he quoting someone?

"But we survive," insisted Atomos. "What's—"

"The island makes us survive," interjected Apollodorus. "What do shadows have to do with that?" This perspective reminded Atomos of Pueo and the fire pit.

Croak!

"I've read about it. The gas coming out of the volcano acts like a hydrothermal vent, heating the Gyre, or something; that's how we survive."

"Or something?" questioned Atomos.

"Listen!" shouted Apollodorus. "Nobody even knows where we are, much less how we got here. None of these scrolls say, not one. Go ahead. Look around yourself. I assure you, no map, not anywhere, can tell us where on earth the Gyre is. Maybe we're even under Antarctica." He shrugged. "The ancient Atlanteans must've wanted this place kept secret a lot more than we know."

"What about the shadow?" insisted Atomos.

"Who's to say it's the Leviathan? To me, the shadow seems a lot more similar to the ancient Japanese myth of the Umibozu."

"Who?" asked Atomos.

"The Umibozu," repeated Apollodorus. "Looking down on sailors in the dead of night with massive eyes and a smiling face, the great ocean spirit would ask them, 'Do you fear me?' If the sailors responded, 'No,' the Umibozu would disappear, but if the sailors were to say 'Yes,' the Umibozu would devour their ship whole. Granted, some say the legends are based on giant sea turtles, but how far does that get us? Me, I think they're just a mixture of storm clouds and unconscious psychology."

Atomos walked around, pacing through the moss-covered library. Was this Pueo's fate? Had he been swallowed by a giant sea monster? Fiction and nonfiction seemed only a matter of perspective under the shadow of the mermaid gargoyles.

Trees and bushes stuck through gaps in the brick wall. Atomos brushed them with his fingers as he paced the room. "You know, this place sure could use a lot of repairs. Mother Nature hasn't been very kind—"

"It's lasted this long." Apollodorus shrugged again, interrupting. This time, however, he paused in reflection.

In truth, Atomos hated anthropomorphism, or logic that entertained the notion of elemental forces taking on human shape and reason. Why did anyone believe in the supposed mystery of the twelve constellations? Obviously, this was a consequence of humanity's limited modes of storytelling. What difference did it make if, during the winter solstice, for three days, the sun was in the sky fewer hours? Father Time was most always indifferent, almost never passing into a new age, avoiding violence. However, the illusion of his passing changed, astronomically, based on longitude and latitude. The Gyre had no sun. Every day was an equinox. Sure, humans saw seven heavenly beings in the sky: the Sun, Mercury, Venus,[4] the Moon, Mars, Jupiter, and Saturn.[5] Seven! But was this better than twelve? In the Gyre, there were none. There was a shadow.

"Are these holes from a battle?" asked Atomos. "How did they get here?" He knelt to pick up a stone. Swiftly, he used the stone to slice through a tree trunk. Gooey sap bled out from its core. Atomos sniffed the oozing liquid.

"They're from the Warring Period," mumbled Apollodorus over his shoulder. He was so antisocial. *Doesn't he care how the others see him? Is he psychotic or some kind of sociopath?* Apollodorus moved on from showing Atomos around in the scroll room to another section of the library where he showed off busted statues wearing plated armor. "Note the intricacies of the chain mail. Before the advent of Kthulu, the Atlanteans warriors used thinner, less box-shaped armor. The change was made for bows and spears.

---

4   Couldn't be a coincidence why that awful girl was named after not only the hottest planet in the solar system but also the densest.

5   As the father of Jupiter, the king of the gods, Saturn transcended the Roman harvest festival of Saturnalia to become the modern world's weekly holiday, by far the most celebrated and well remembered. People forget, however, that the other six days are named after the sky as well. Sunday and Monday are obvious. The rest can only be understood through the lens of Norse mythology. Jupiter becoming Thor, for example, explains Thursday. Friday and Freya also work.

Definitely more than just a little problem to have while mounted on flying dragons." Atomos didn't care about the so-called history of a sport. "This is the helmet of Raijin, whose cult followers have lit the Gyre with fire from the volcano, ritualistically, for generations. Notice the change in style." The librarian pointed to a statue with all red armor and a gold crescent moon lying horizontally, like horns on its brow.

"I'm going to go walk around upstairs, check it out."

"That's fine," replied Apollodorus, nonchalant. "Go ahead. Poke around."

Atomos reveled in this opportunity to be alone. He wasn't going to wait around for the librarian to change his mind. If he found a gold ring in the tower, he'd want it for himself. Atomos climbed the winding staircases until, eventually, he reached the highest room. However, it was not full of treasure as Atomos had hoped. Instead, a mirror stood in the center of the room on wooden floorboards. The shine he'd seen outside must have reflected off the mirror's gold frame.

As Atomos got closer, stepping into the frame, he saw himself, standing in front of a mirror. His muscles were toned and defined. Back home, he only had a single mirror, and it was so smushed he could barely see a thing in it. What a skewed perception of himself he'd had.

Leaning in, Atomos saw his scar above his lip and frowned. Then he leaned back, stepped in further still, and flexed in the mirror. He wished the years would pass more quickly. As they did, surely he'd grow bigger. The body and mind were moldable, he reassured himself. Atomos raised his chin and puffed out his chest, imagining it twice as large as it was presently.

On the gold frame above, Atomos read the inscription: *NEVE RO DDO REVEN*. These weren't indiscernible scribblings like Atomos had seen on the fountain. The letters were English, like they'd been on the scrolls. Still, the words were foreign to him. In his head, they sounded as if they could be elvish or perhaps some language of the fairies. At once Atomos remembered that in a mirror, everything was backward. Neverod and doreven were the same forward and backward. *Never odd or even.*

It was a palindrome, although the true meaning behind the words was hidden. The inscription was clearly a riddle. Atomos wondered, *What is never odd or even? Every number is either odd or even—well, all numbers except for zero. Wait! Is the answer that simple?* He wasn't even sure if he believed in the concept; all the same, he didn't have to prove anything.

Atomos dropped his eyes back to the mirror and saw himself once more, an athletic young man with freckles and shaggy ginger hair. He twitched his nose and his scarred upper lip, but then, quite curiously, his left eyebrow raised, wrinkling his forehead. Atomos couldn't tell if he'd done that on purpose. His face did weird stuff now and again. He winced. Then, Atomos raised his right hand. To his great surprise, the mirror image in front of him also raised its hand, only on the other side—that is, it did not raise the opposite hand a mirror was supposed to raise. If this mirror wasn't reflecting reality, what was it doing?

Clouds were coming behind his mirror self. He extended his hand toward himself—not toward his double's hand, but his chest and shoulder. Atomos applied pressure to the reflection, and doing this, he felt no resistance. Atomos pushed his hand directly through the invisible pane. His doppelgänger did the same. Together, they smiled. Atomos placed his hand over the other's heart. Again, he felt no resistance. Once more, Atomos pushed through. The reflection standing in front of him disappeared, fading into mist. Behind his outstretched hand, Atomos saw nobody. Instead, he now saw the cold, black mountain where he'd first seen the four guardians rise on their dragons out of the sea: Trash Island.

Atomos saw the sun behind the mountain, moving across the sky with the clouds, again and again. Then, in a rapid procession, a series of ships arrived, docking around the base of the floating black island. From a distance, humans like him, dressed in shiny yellow-and-orange raincoats, swarmed the mountain almost like ants. The machines on their backs sucked up the surface of black rock, revealing color after color underneath. Before long, the floating mountain looked like contemporary art.

Then, the men left. After their boats were gone, the colorful floating mountain shrank and shrank, until it was almost flat, spreading out further and further. But this wasn't a single, lonely hill anymore. The massive, colorful island was no longer alone in the water. Instead, in every direction, Atomos saw hills of mismatched colors, every shape and size. Every color known to man was floating out there in the ocean. Atomos noticed the trash moved together like the flow of the waves. He reached out, toward the handlebars of a rusty brown bicycle, but it pulled away from him. *Damn!* All the trash seemed to be swirling, spinning counterclockwise. Atomos was in the middle of a maelstrom. Even the clouds above him were caught in a spiral.

Then, suddenly, another ship arrived. This ship was alone and pushed through the cracks of the floating islands. Then the boat docked as close to Atomos as it possibly could. It was Pueo's boat! Atomos was positive. From inside, the rotund Hawaiian peered his head out. Then, he climbed off his boat and walked backward, toward Atomos. This was strange, he thought; Pueo never usually walked backward. Was he seeing time in reverse? How far did it go? Would he see humans turn to fish? Maybe he'd witness the most famous of them all at the rebirth of time itself, in the last age, before Aquarius. Still, Atomos was more curious about what Pueo was holding in his hands. He couldn't get a good look. Pueo's black hair was far too long.

In a single, swift motion, Pueo turned to reveal a baby. It was Atomos! He was a baby, ginger hair and all, held up by an ankle. Pueo wiped the baby off with his clothes and knelt down to the trash below. Setting the baby down, headfirst, Pueo let go. In and among the garbage, the baby Atomos sank into the vortex. All that was visible of him was his tiny little foot. Pueo got back up. He walked away backward again; this time, however, he faced Atomos in the mirror. What had Atomos just seen? Was that how it had actually happened? Pueo hadn't found him in a net like he'd always said?

"Atomos," yelled Apollodorus.

10

ACHILLES'S HELIX

Apollodorus dragged Atomos out by his neck and shoulders. Leaning heavily into the mirror, his body had been almost entirely inside. Apollodorus had no reservations about plunking his own arms in to grab the human. In the deepest corners of his imagination, Atomos still wondered what it was he saw: was that the light, the darkness, the truth? As the last of his face withdrew from the pane, his reflection reformed, and Atomos looked at himself differently. Could this side of him turn around his way of thinking? There was desperation in his own gray eyes. Was that even him? Was he a shadow of the past, or did history simply give his character more color?

"You found the mirror!" exclaimed Apollodorus, ecstatic. "Or, perhaps, in hindsight, it might be more accurate to say the mirror found you." Apollodorus touched the golden frame, rubbing it curiously with his fingers. "That reminds me. Atomos, you're human."

"Yes?" replied Atomos suspiciously. Was that even a question?

"I was thinking," asked Apollodorus, distracted, "you're not interested

in reading my copy of *History and Consequence of the Red Square*, are you?"
He held out a scroll tied with a red ribbon.

"No. I'm good," answered Atomos, feeling as though he'd seen enough
red for a lifetime. "But I don't understand, Apollodorus. How did it 'find'
me?"

"Have you ever heard of a Venus flytrap before?" asked Apollodorus.

"Yes, I have," responded Atomos. "It's that spiky plant that eats bugs
and traps them with its teeth. It's native to America, right?"

"Great! You've heard of it," he shouted. "Most of the Atlanteans have
never left the Gyre, so they never know. Morphology is very hard stuff to
explain to people living on an island that always stays the same. Science is
dead here. Almost like you just were." He laughed nervously. "Well, you
know what I mean? The mirror is like that carnivorous plant in how it
catches its prey. Tiny hairs on each plant called trigger hairs feel the prey."

Atomos drifted out for a second. He was bored by anything and
everything Apollodorus had to say. He noticed, out of the tower's window,
a shining, almost rainbow-colored dragon flying through the mountains,
over the jungle. Its iridescent tail was long and luxurious. *That's odd*,
thought Atomos. He didn't recognize this dragon at all. Weren't only the
guardians allowed to take their dragons out of the dragon encampment
before the games?

"Once the trap snaps shut," Apollodorus continued, "the carnivore
devours its prey, but only if another point of contact is triggered. The
mirror—I mean, the Venus plant—wants to avoid trapping objects with
no nutritional value; after that, the slow process of digestion begins."

"Venus? Like the guardian?" muttered Atomos, still gazing out the
window. Was that who he'd seen? No. Her dragon was matte white.

"My cousin? No, definitely not. I hate her! God, why'd you have to
say that? She'd be staring at this mirror all day. What? Do you like her?
Who are you to her, her new Adonis? Damn! Now look at what you've
done. I won't be able to get the image out of my head. I won't ever be able
to see this mirror the same." The librarian's eyes glimmered as he turned
toward himself, hypocritically. He stared at his own reflection all the same.

"So, the mirror preys on people who look too deep?" asked Atomos.

"Yes!" Apollodorus beamed. "You understand."

"Yeah, I get it. It uses hypnosis to hunt." This was exactly like the cuttlefish. He couldn't take being around such an arrogant know-it-all anymore. "I have the scrolls now, so I don't need you anymore, Apollodorus. I'm just going to continue on my own. Don't lose your pet again." Atomos knew he was responding irrationally. He'd just block it from his mind for now. He didn't need a teacher, not now, not ever. Nature had taught him enough.

"No worries," answered the librarian, who went back to distantly gazing into the mirror. Atomos wondered what Apollodorus saw in the distance when he looked beyond his own self. Maybe he didn't see anything. Perhaps, he considered, Apollodorus had yet to work out the *zero* clue. Just as he was thinking this, though, Atomos was corrected. "I'll be fine. I've done this plenty. You go."

Atomos had a sneaking suspicion that, in some way, Apollodorus wasn't telling him the whole truth. He left regardless. "Aloha!"

Turning his back from the library as he left, Atomos envisioned how terrible it'd be to be sent back without Azure. What if the golden ring didn't take him home, but somewhere random? How would he get back? He was halfway across the world. Without a dragon, he'd need to swim. Hopefully, it wouldn't be an issue. All he needed to do was not break any rules.

Apollodorus was breeding dragons. He didn't care about the Oceanic Contract. Telling the knights, however, would be unwise. Never do that to a friend. Although no friend is like any other, all have strength that is one's own weakness and vice versa. A common goal draws them together. Fighting and constant conflict are good. But it only works if they go through it together. Sometimes, the strongest lifelong friendships happen over a week. Other times, you can be friends with someone for a lifetime and still not know them. Atomos thought of Pueo.

If he was going to be alone, it would be because that's what he chose, not because anyone else left him. Atomos thought of snapping a few tree branches. There weren't any clean breaks in life. *Get out while you're ahead, come up for air*—that's all he could think. Still there was no relief. Atomos trekked through the jungle, stepping over more branches, boulders, logs, and the odd vine. Again, it astonished him that the trees were so bare in comparison to those back home on the island. But unlike the burned roots left behind in America's deforested tropics, this jungle felt truly alive.

Atomos reached the top of a tall peak. From this vantage point, he could see everything in the Gyre: the volcano, the knights' courtyard, the dragon encampment in the center of the lake, even the beach where he'd first stumbled and fallen on his face. The infamous arena he saw far off in the distance, partially covered by hills. Atomos wondered if he'd ever see Achilles's final resting spot. At this point, was it even worth his time? Time had flown so quickly since coming to the Gyre. Everything about the past twenty-four hours ran together.

A strange, bittersweet feeling of preemptive nostalgia crossed his mind. Would Atomos forget how it felt to stand in the Gyre? He tried to take a mental picture of the rolling hills in his mind. Did being happy always mean being sad afterward? Hopefully, he'd be able to remember the rest of the Isle of Immortals, too, long after he was gone. The Knights' Vortex Prayer, or whatever it was called, Atomos decided he could forget; that'd be fine with him. What was a vortex anyway? A sphere? A cylinder? A cone? Did it spiral or corkscrew? Did it grow and move on, or just barrel forward? Did it rotate around a center? Was it a helix?

Suddenly, Atomos noticed from across the Gyre the same sparkling, pearly-white, multicolored dragon he'd seen earlier, flying into a cave inside the tallest mountain on the island. Who rode this opaline dragon? Why were they hiding in a cave before the games? Could this be the location of the golden ring? Atomos started sprinting down the hill, bounding toward the cave. Before he made it more than halfway, however, Atomos ran into Titania, the guardian, knocking her to the ground. Their heads collided and they fell, tumbling down the hillside.

11
BEYOND THE OUTER RIM

Over some boulders and through some trees, sliding downhill, breaking branches and snapping twigs, Atomos and Titania landed off to the side of the main path where they'd been walking. They each picked themselves off the ground with haste. Leaves and pebbles stuck to their faces. The triangle shape of their imprint remained in the ground. The tangle of green hands had left white stripes on their faces, quickly turning pink.

"I'm sorry. I didn't mean to—" began Atomos, holding his hands up. Titania held up hers as well. She didn't want to hear it. Nothing he could say would matter; however, that too didn't matter. Atomos didn't say anything at all. For the first time since they'd met, he saw the guardian up close and was captivated by how beautiful the black-haired princess was. Titania had no armor on, wearing only her black robe. Hers had no highlights at all. Perhaps they too were covered in dirt. They had just both fallen in a ditch and probably rolled a good ten feet through the mud. They were lucky neither had hit their head on any of the protruding boulders or tree stumps.

"What was that for?" growled Titania, picking leaves out of her tangled, black braid. "Are you . . . Damn, look what you've done, you— you stupid human! Can't take my brother in a fair fight, so what? You ambush a girl?"

"I said I didn't mean to," repeated Atomos. "What're you doing here?"

"I was on my way to the library, not that it's any of your business."

Atomos felt very intimidated by the princess. Titania's dark hair and muscular build reminded him a little too much of Oberon. Atomos climbed swiftly out of the ditch. Then, he knelt down and offered her his hand. She accepted, but not without a soft groan and a roll of her eyes.

"Were you looking for a scroll?" he asked. Atomos pulled Titania from the ditch, placing her firmly back on her feet.

"I wanted to borrow a few from the founders. Why do you care? What was it, Achilles?"

Atomos didn't answer.

"Or should I call you Little Prince? That's you, right? Prince of the mermaids?" There was more than a touch of sarcasm and resentment in her tone.

"I don't know about this 'prince' business. You're not really going to call me that, are you? Do I look the part?" Atomos gestured to his clothes—or, rather, lack thereof. Titania couldn't care less. "I've never met my parents. Think that's going to be a problem?" Titania turned away from him. He placed his hands inside the pockets of his cargo shorts, suddenly not quite so confident. "So yeah, I was following a shining white dragon to a cave."

Somewhat out of character, Titania seemed interested in what Atomos had to say, or at least the last bit. Still, after this momentary lapse, her face reverted back to its normal expressionlessness.

Unfazed by the silence, Atomos continued, "None of you rode a sparkling dragon. I know it's not Vulcan. Do you know who else it might be or where they might be going?"

"You're talking about Vulcan's twin sister. Apollo rides her now," responded Titania. Atomos sensed a hint of contempt in her words.

"Apollo?" questioned Atomos, unsure. "You mean Apollodorus? No way. It can't be. I was just with him."

"No, not Apollodorus. Apollo! He's Agathon's right hand. Don't you remember? He yelled at you in the courtyard." Atomos did remember. "Apollo has been on the Isle of Immortals nearly as long as Agathon. They must be up to something." Titania seemed very distant, staring off toward the stripes of the Gyre overhead. The sky here was always the same. Why, all of a sudden, was she now so transfixed? Atomos stayed quiet. Suddenly, Titania turned to him. "I want to go with you. I want you to show me where this cave is."

"Yeah, sure," Atomos agreed. He had a feeling she'd be helpful in directing him to the cave. "Let's get out of here."

They started walking on the path that led down the hill. For Titania, this was back the same direction she'd come. "Wait. Hold on." Atomos stopped in his tracks. "Don't you have to go to the library? Didn't you want to see Apollodorus? You came all the way here."

"It can wait," replied Titania. "Although I need to talk to Apollodorus soon. Hopefully, he'll just be his usual hermit self and keep his head down."

"What was it you were going to tell him?" asked Atomos.

"My brother," she began. "He's been banished." This news took Atomos by surprise. Titania continued, "After you left, Agathon and Venus turned the tables on Oberon. They accused him of plotting to overthrow the knights and kill Agathon. Zagreus refused to take anyone's side."

"What did you do?" he asked. Atomos lowered his hand toward the ground, insisting that Titania lead the way. Chivalry felt so much better in books, but all the reading in the world couldn't have hidden the fact that he'd never done this before. Atomos had to stop himself from shaking. Titania eyed Atomos suspiciously.

"I left. What else was there?" Atomos felt the pain in Titania's voice, far removed from its characteristic monotone. He knew that although her question was rhetorical and her tone defensive, she was honest and sincere. It was clear from her expression, even without her nervously tugging at her hair. Atomos figured he shouldn't press the issue.

"A few hours later, I came back, but the trial was over. The council had found him guilty." Titania raised her voice. "I wanted to talk to him, to anyone, but I couldn't. I couldn't get caught."

"Yeah? So? Oberon's banished. So was Apollodorus. It's fine."

"Apollodorus was only excommunicated," returned Titania cautiously. "Participating in the Knight's Prayer is more than just drinking from a fountain. He'll die in the Gyre, more likely sooner rather than later."

Atomos ignored this last comment. He didn't want to start back in on a whole other tangent.

"Where's Oberon?" he inquired, persistent.

"The knights sent him back to the surface world, permanently."

"What do you mean? How can they do that?"

"Agathon holds the power. At first, when he returned, Oberon placed himself at the mercy of the council. He thought Agathon would support his obvious victory." Titania paused, smiling. "No offense."

"None taken," he sighed.

Titania continued, "Agathon took Oberon's green ring to prevent him from returning. Then, he used the power of the gold ring to send him to the surface."

"Where exactly? The ruins? Did his dragon go with him?"

"Why do you care?" she said. "Not since Triton has any dragon been banished alongside their rider. Actually, I named my own dragon, Tyrian, in honor of his companion. Legend says he was one of the first dragons to be given their own name, a glorious shade of purple."

"Tyrian?" questioned Atomos. "Like tyranny?"

"That's very Hellenistic," judged the guardian. Atomos didn't follow. "Before their conflict with Alexander the Great, the seafaring people of Tyre or the Phoenicians of Byblos were the first race of humans to explore the Mediterranean. They caught Tyrian sea snails off the shores of modern-day Turkey, Lebanon, Israel, and Syria. They were no tyrants. You had a Bronze Age because of them."

"It's just a saying," said Atomos apologetically. He wondered again what had happened to her gold armor, although he thought it best not to ask.

"The Phoenicians were traders and fishermen, but their rampant construction of boats also led to the extinction of all their local trees."

"Like pirates?" questioned Atomos, cupping his right eye. "With an eye?"

"Absolutely not." Atomos had a feeling the two went hand in hand. "They were masters of industry, creators of all phonetic languages. The people of Tyre harvested their snails to make a dye that never grows old and never looks tired. What's the matter with that?" Nearby leaves shook violently. Beams of light danced all over the forest floor, beside the rocks and leaves, to the left and right off the path. Suddenly, from behind them, a tremendous black dragon soared over the thick jungle trees. Titania glanced up.

"What's—"

"Hey! That's Osiris! That's Oberon's dragon." Titania turned sharply on her heels. "Please, can't you . . . Uh, uh . . . Thomas, please, here. Lift me onto your shoulders." She crawled onto his back. "I need to see who's flying my brother's dragon."

"I'll do you one better," he replied, confident despite the fact that Titania still didn't know his name. After lifting her onto his shoulders, he climbed up a sturdy palm tree. Atomos wondered whether Titania had thought he was young like the others. When he looked up at her, however, she maintained a stern expression. Was this ambivalence or apathy? Whatever it was, the expression was like a mask. Her coy silence was anything but shallow. "Are you okay?"

"It's Agathon and Venus," she said, regretful. "Let me down, Atomos. I know where we're going. Let's keep walking."

"Okay," replied Atomos happily. He lifted Titania over his head and gently set her back down on her feet again. They walked for what felt like hours, saying nothing, but after a while, Titania began to reveal her true feelings.

"We need change, Atomos. Everyone's so focused on keeping the Gyre a secret, but is that really the best thing we could be doing? The only reason you're here is you're a dragon rider." Titania then gave Atomos a sharply critical look. "Allegedly," she added, smiling. Atomos was embarrassed.

"I thought the Gyre was supposed to be society at its best?" He smiled awkwardly.

"Truth is, in my opinion, your world doesn't want to become more like the Gyre." Titania and Atomos stepped out of the lush, green forest. "I want this place to be more like the way yours was before."

Suddenly, they were surrounded by pools of water. An overflowing lake blocked them from persisting.

"My island isn't so bad," said Atomos. "Hawaiians are different from other people. You would know if you asked."

Titania ignored him. She didn't have time for distractions. "Nothing's ever enough, is it?" she sighed. "It's the path of all humans. You always want more and, what's worse, you've accepted it. Maybe not you specifically, but still, I'm sure you've seen firsthand what I'm talking about."

Along the rocky bank that separated the trees from the water, Atomos saw a cliff hanging out over a small patch of open land, size enough for only one dragon, maybe two. Focusing his eyes and ears above the top of the cliff, Atomos heard a deep roar coming from the high cave.

Titania grabbed his wrist from behind. "Atomos! Hide!" She pulled them into a nearby bush. The black dragon, Osiris, came jetting out of the cave with Agathon and Venus on its back.

"So, it's just Apollo up there now?" asked Atomos.

"He has a dragon, Atomos. You don't. Did you forget that?"

"What do you want us to do, then?" responded Atomos impatiently.

"We'll wait for Apollo to leave too. Each morning, Agathon's prized marksman rides the outer rim with his white dragon, flies to the top of the Gyre, and uses his flaming arrow to illuminate the sky."

"Apollo ignites the sky with fire? How can the wave be so bright? The sun is a hundred times wider than Earth. I don't understand. How can a man-made fire stay lit underwater?"

"Well, first of all, the Gyre isn't man-made."

"Touché."

"Secondly, haven't you noticed the big wave's been getting darker?"

Atomos thought back. He hadn't gazed upon the wave much, but of the shadows he'd seen, those from this morning had been much darker. Maybe it was all in his head. None had any grown longer, obviously. However, earlier, there'd been more colors on the leaves and bushes. The lake, too, had been black.

Titania continued, "The algae living along the outer rim is bioluminescent. Apollo's arrow isn't really flaming. It does, however, create a chemical reaction that envelops the sky and produces enough light for the entire island. Each day, the algae will all burn off over ten hours; then, each night, it regrows."

"Ten hours! Aren't your years the same as ours? How long are your nights? How many Atlantean days are in an Atlantean year?"

"Atlanteans only remember our connection to the sun to mark time since we were last absorbed in its light. What other reason do we have to divide time into members and nonmembers?"

"You don't think you're chosen?"

Titania didn't answer. She pointed past the cliff to the water and the horizon. "There, that's how we'll wait," she said finally.

Atomos didn't know at all what she meant. Was she flat-out ignoring him? Was this how all Atlanteans acted? What on earth did she mean?

"I'm confused," confessed Atomos. Titania beamed, gazing back at him. This was the first time he'd ever seen her happy.

"Atomos, I'm going to take you to the outer rim."

"Should we leave now?"

"Let's give it an hour or two."

"What should we do until then? What's on your mind?"

"Nothing." Titania sounded like she was lying. She squatted in the sand.

"Why don't you tell me about the founders?" he asked.

"Apollodorus is the one who told me, but what he said is that, in the beginning, there was a man called Prometheus who was famous for molding humankind from rocks and water with his brother, Epimetheus."

"Rocks are mortal?" Atomos was half joking.

"Aren't they? They have veins. Does that make them or trees any less immortal?"

"Trees or rocks?"

"Either. It doesn't make sense to me to create walls over death, but instead to create monuments of life."

"How did he do it?"

"Who?" she asked.

"Prometheus."

"Only two survivors were said to have escaped the disastrous great flood. Prometheus was the first. The second, however, was not the brother, Epimetheus, who, just as expected, was late, but his brother's wife, Pandora, offering Prometheus a chance to escape in her floating box."

"Hence the name of the story."

"They floated for weeks, together, through the ocean. Birds of prey stalked them. Prometheus never slept. He didn't want his eyes plucked out. Clinging together in the pouring rain, shivering and chattering, only two things entered their minds: hope or despair. However, they were really one and the same. One morning, while gazing at a star, the man saw a vision and, far off in the distance, caught a glimpse of their combined future. In addition to life, Pandora gave him the greatest gift of all: love."

"Love?" repeated Atomos in disbelief.

"That's the way the story goes," she said, shrugging off the association. "What it really means is that the island of dragons prevented them both from growing old or sustaining injuries, so long as they each continued to live there forevermore."

"I understand."

It was nearly dark. Atomos and Titania had waited for the perfect time to move without being seen. Each kicked their feet through the sand, having walked along the beach and past the cliff. Each had tiny surfboards under their arms. Atomos had carved them himself from the trees. Titania stood a few feet in front, pointing to the edge of the Gyre.

"The water's going to be very loud, so just follow me and watch what I do when we get there," insisted Titania. "Are you ready?"

Atomos nodded when she turned back. The whole scene reminded

Atomos of the last time Pueo and he had gone surfing together. However, this time, it was he who was hanging back, pondering life, not Pueo.

"Will we be back before Apollo leaves?" asked Atomos nervously, but Titania was too far away to hear him. She was not shy when it came to paddling through the surf. Atomos stuck the nose of his board into the water, perpendicular to the horizon. When he glanced up, it occurred to Atomos that here in the Gyre, the horizon wasn't really a horizon after all. The edge moved so much that it was relatively indiscernible, perhaps even nonexistent. The closer he got, the higher the wave appeared. Then, Atomos had an idea: what if all horizons were imaginary? The idea of a flat line was already an illusion, he was sure. The world was a round ball. The eye of the beholder is, and has always been, too limited. Perhaps, though, he'd simply never been close enough to the horizon. Was it even possible to be perpendicular to a circle? He imagined looking down from a bird's-eye view, paddling out to sea. Wasn't that a radius? Atomos thought back to his math textbooks tucked away in his and Pueo's hut. Wavelengths, that's all he could remember. Before long, Atomos realized it didn't matter. He was caught in a tangent.

"Wait up," yelled Atomos desperately. A large wave crashed over his head. Again, Atomos got no answer from Titania. She paddled onward, toward the outer rim. Meanwhile, the waves pushed back against them. Sometimes they hit the underside of his board, sending Atomos up and over the rising waves. Other times, the waves straight up slapped him in the face. The cold water dripped down his hair and jawline, then pulled Atomos forward into the next dip. Where was this energy coming from? One moment, the water drifted without care, the next it twisted and turned in a vicious torrent. Atomos was nervous. His makeshift boards surely wouldn't hold up to the power of the Gyre. If its pull was anything like the doorway in the Atlantean temple, he'd be in for the ride of his life.

Not even at the height of that hurricane the night Azure had been blown onto his island had Atomos ever seen weather like this. Never before had one giant, ongoing wave spanned his entire view. The most troublesome aspect of that occasion, Atomos remembered, had been Mother Nature's cruel persistence. Here, however, nothing ever seemed to stay in one place long enough to make any discernible change. The outer rim was an example of Mother Nature and Father Time coming together as one, even more than the horizon back home. Standing on their boards, facing back toward the island, Atomos raised his arms above his head as they ascended the wave. He felt at one with the all-encompassing Gyre, lifting his palms to the sky.

Titania laughed. "What are you doing?"

Atomos couldn't hear. The rushing water was too loud. The bluish glow of the Gyre was dull, much darker than it'd been only minutes earlier. Now, however, because they were so close to its surface, Atomos and Titania could see themselves in the low light. At last, Atomos understood why she'd compared the Gyre's aura to the sun. When Atomos glanced at Titania, riding a few feet above him, he saw her expression quickly change in the mystic cyan light. Despite her hostile eyes, she'd been staring at him too, accidentally, caught in a daydream. She pointed to her hand. Atomos stared down at his own, covered in freckles.

"No." Titania shook her arms, trying to catch his attention. Then, she pointed to her hand again and leaned back on her surfboard. Bubbles jetted above her. Atomos was impressed. He stuck his hand into the Gyre's outer rim but was surprised to feel that, unlike the warm waters of the South Pacific, the water beneath the surface went from being a little cold to feeling like actual ice. His legs, hands, and wrists were all immersed in the water. He hadn't come all this way not to push on. Atomos pressed against the Gyre with all his might, expecting more bubbles to jet out around his forearm. Nothing happened. It was impenetrable. Exactly like the Atlantean doorway, the fervent wave was only a few inches thick and splashed water everywhere, soaking Atomos. No matter how much he tried, however, Atomos couldn't push his hand past the barrier. He tried harder.

As they climbed the wave, now nearly fifty feet from where they'd been only seconds earlier, Atomos felt the cold exterior of the Gyre underneath his palm. Was this the water shifting and moving? Was this a natural curve? No, this was different. Ever so slightly, Atomos felt the ice-cold barrier pulling away from his palm and his fingertips. His teeth were chattering. Atomos clenched his jaw. Then, it dawned on him: the Gyre was widening. Once more, Titania caught his attention, waving her arms. She pointed back toward the island, to the mountaintop. They'd almost climbed high enough to see over it. As Atomos focused, he saw Apollo's white dragon leaving the cave. The glistening of its scales was unmistakable.

Nosediving, they glided down the wave while Apollo flew over the jungle, toward the volcano by the courtyard. Atomos chased after Titania. He hoped the two of them wouldn't be seen. Without his dragon, this edge was probably the most vulnerable place for him. Perhaps he shouldn't have been so quick to trust Titania. Still, nothing bad had come of it—not yet.

Apollo and his dragon reached the volcano, and the hot air from the volcano lifted them. The pair ascended higher than Atomos could even imagine, toward the top of the Gyre. Atomos wouldn't have been able to see if Apollo's dragon hadn't been so dazzlingly reflective. Finally, the two surfers paddled inland.

"Titania, why can't I push past the outer rim?" asked Atomos when she was within earshot. "Apollodorus told me that King Triton—"

"Save your questions, Atomos," interrupted Titania as they walked out of the waist-high water and up to the sandy beach. "We don't have much time." Atomos scanned the cliffside. The rocks were dispersed, but nothing too bad. He'd climbed worse with a whale on his back. After turning back around, Atomos beamed at Titania, who'd stooped down to fix her braid.

Despite her typical apathetic tone, Atomos knew she'd agree when he said, "You're right, Titania. We do need change."

Again, they looked upward. Atomos started to climb.

12

THE DARKEST CAVE

There are very few things in this life that are truly hard, thought Atomos. *Losing Pueo has been hard. Would losing Azure feel the same?* Atomos struggled to come to terms with the idea that he'd never see the old fisherman again. His eyes began to water. Atomos wiped his tears on his bicep. How was he so weak? What if Titania saw him crying? Most things were simply challenging, he resolved. *One way or another, you need to think on your feet—unless you're a cephalopod.* That was just an expression for them. Atomos looked down at his own feet, dangling in midair. What use was that advice in Kthulu? He was giving this thought too much weight. *Think like an octopus,* thought Atomos.

"Are you sure it's safe for you to be here?" he asked as Titania climbed along beside him. She seemed genuinely puzzled by this question as she lifted herself up onto a ledge on the cliffside.

"What do you mean?" asked Titania.

"Didn't you say you couldn't be caught by Agathon and the knights? What if they find you? Can't you leave?" Atomos climbed up beside her on the ledge.

"Atomos, the real reason I'm still here isn't because I don't care about my brother," said Titania, leaping to the next rock to grab onto. She caught her breath. "The games are in two days. I don't have anywhere else to go. I don't think that'll ever change. But like we said before . . ." She studied him with a gleam in her black eyes. "Change is good."

Titania reached for another rock above her head and pulled herself up. Atomos was baffled. He wondered about what *we* could possibly mean, but thought it best not to pay it too much attention.

They mounted the final edge of the cliffside. Finally, the entrance lay at their feet. The cave was not very deep, perhaps twenty or thirty feet. Atomos was surprised. No dragon could get inside, not even Azure, the smallest of them all. Slowly, walking side by side, the pair wandered down the dark corridor.

"You don't think anyone is still here, do you?" whispered Atomos.

"No. I doubt it," Titania answered. "Look, over there!" She pointed to a circular room at the end of the tunnel. "It's the gold ring!" Sitting on a table at the end of the cave, Atomos could just barely make it out from the shimmer.

"Should we?" asked Atomos nervously.

"Go on, grab it." Just as those words escaped Titania's mouth, what little light coming into the cave from outside was completely cut out. Everything was pitch black.

Atomos hid the ring in his pocket. "Someone's here." He hid behind a crevice in the rocky, misshapen wall.

"Hello, Titania, I didn't expect to see you here."

Although it was too dark to see, Atomos instantly recognized the low, discomforting voice.

"Agathon," answered Titania nervously. "I didn't expect to see you riding my brother's dragon after his banishment. Don't you have one of your own?"

"Surprise, surprise," he remarked.

"Where's Venus? I thought she was with you now."

Atomos breathed a sigh of relief he wasn't who Titania was upset with.

"She's at the dragon encampment," Agathon answered calmly. "More importantly, though"—Agathon slid off the back of the black dragon and hit the ground; *thump!*—"have you come here to steal the ring?

"I would never," denied Titania, characteristically emotionless.

"You're part of Oberon's rebellion, aren't you? Of course you are. To think, the Oceanic Contract used to be upheld by you two so-called guardians. How do I know you won't bring him back? He conspired to have me killed, Titania!"

"I'm not here to say anything about my brother's crimes," countered Titania. "But you know what, Agathon, it's you who should be put on trial. That's one thing I will say."

"On trial for what?" he laughed. Atomos wondered how close they were standing to each other now. "I've dedicated my life to the Isle of Immortals," growled Agathon. "My path is chosen for me; the Leviathan has foreseen this. Every action I make is because I am towed in its wake. The feelings I receive are halfway between thinking and dreaming. I admit, the original intent is sometimes difficult to decipher, but that's not my main concern."

"Maybe it should be," she snapped.

"Do you question my authority as an interpreter?"

"Corruption, Agathon. That's your crime." Atomos had no trouble hearing Titania's sassy voice. "You've pitted the knights and the guardians against each other to cover up the destruction of the library. Oberon told me. Only you've been here since the Cult Period! You were behind the feuds. You used the power of the council to form a new government, you and you alone!"

"There is no government in Gyre, you silly girl. Have you ever paid taxes?"

"Don't touch me," Titania cried. Atomos couldn't see what was happening, but he felt the impulse to go out there and defend her. At the same time, however, he remembered the way she'd thrown the rope over Azure, surfed down the wave, and climbed up the mountain at the same pace as, if not faster, than him. Titania could handle herself. Plus, Atomos didn't want to give away his position to Agathon. *She must be planning something. Why else would she have waited until now, with nobody around, to confront Agathon?*

"Why, Titania? Are you trying to be excommunicated like your friend the librarian? Do you want to be banished like your brother?"

Atomos could tell, even from where he was standing, this was hard for Titania to hear.

"What reason could I possibly have for wanting that?"

Agathon ignored her question. Atomos couldn't tell—was she being sarcastic?

"You and I both know, if there is going to be an excommunication, a council meeting has to be held and all the knights must be present," uttered the skeptic. "Where's my gold ring? You're trying to steal it, aren't you?"

Atomos felt a bead of sweat roll down his forehead.

"Why would I want to be excommunicated right before the games? Are you going crazy? I don't deny the existence of Leviathan. All this power's gone to your head, Agathon."

"You haven't answered my question," shouted Agathon angrily.

"I never saw a ring," she answered. "I was searching for Apollo." For once, Atomos heard raw emotion in her voice.

"My other question," the knight snapped. "I don't care what you do or don't deny. Answer me!" Titania gave no reply. "You know about the reformations. Now, come with me."

Atomos heard no resistance from Titania. He thought he would've at least heard them getting on the dragon, but nothing.

Thwap! Thwap!

Suddenly, they were gone, and the light coming from outside the cave was stronger than ever. Atomos covered his eyes. The intensity and brightness were blinding. Atomos walked toward it. He held one hand over his face and the other, outstretched into seeming nothingness.

"Atomos? Is that you?" chirped a familiar, friendly voice. It was Venus. Wasn't she supposed to be at the encampment? What was she doing?

Why was she always so nice to him? He didn't get it. Was this another lie? Everyone said they hated her—everyone except Agathon, and the Leviathan, apparently. Atomos didn't understand. How was Venus so terrible?

"Hi, Venus," relented Atomos, unsure and obviously guilty. Atomos had never been very good at lying. Pueo had a much better memory than him and could always piece together the truth, so coming up with lies was out of the question. With a gasp, Atomos felt the ledge shake as a large white dragon landed on its edge, balancing with an unshakable poise. Shards of silver light enveloped the edges of the dragon's shimmering white scales.

"I can't believe my eyes. Why, if it isn't the great human dragon rider. It has been too long, hasn't it? I didn't think I'd be seeing you until you forget you had a dragon again." Venus cackled in a high-pitched, deafening tone. Atomos was now starting to see why she was despised so. She had no remorse. Also, she looked different now. Her long, silver hair was now tied up into a tight bun. She crossed her arms under her breasts. "Tell me, what's it like?"

"What's what like?" Atomos snapped.

"What's it like, human, to have been so close, only to lose everything?" Venus chuckled.

"What do you mean?" questioned Atomos.

"Is freedom really free when you can't leave the Gyre? So, you must not mind turning to stone?"

He laughed, but Atomos was petrified. *Stone?* The end had never really worried him before. In the human world, death was democratic; everybody died. Here, in the Gyre, neither was the case. No death. No democracy. "Are you ready to find out what's after?" he sneered.

"He's trying to steal Agathon's gold ring, Apollo!" Venus said, eager to share this information to spite Atomos. Their friendship had obviously not meant much. She glanced back at Atomos with a strangely sadistic smile. "Did you not hear me, Knight, or should I call you Shining One, Light Bringer, O' Son of the Morning?"

"I understand. No need for boasting, Venus. I'm just astonished. The kid didn't even know the ring had a curse. Isn't that wise?" Venus and Apollo burst into laughter.

Atomos felt terribly humiliated. His plan had all been for nothing.

"Haven't you wondered what'll happen after you stop drinking from the Gyre's water? Didn't you know breathing this air would come at a cost? Even if you were able to find someone to help, to send you back without a ring, you'd still never be able to swim up to the surface from the Atlantean temple before you drown."

"You don't know that. I can swim," objected Atomos.

"That's such a great idea," cheered Venus, helpful as ever. "I love it! Let's send him back ourselves, Apollo. Take the ring from him!"

Atomos grabbed Venus, pinning her arm behind her back.

"Take one more step and she's gone." Without either of the Atlanteans noticing, Atomos had managed to sneak the golden ring onto his finger. Could he actually do it? His eyes were wild and full of rage. His red hair was tossed every which way. Now, he had the power.

"If you do, human, you'll be dead for sure." His jaw clenched, Apollo looked dead serious. "I'll tell Agathon what you've done and you'll die. I promise you that."

"Well then, Knight, I suppose we've reached the point of no return." Atomos coldly stared into the Atlantean's eyes. "Agathon didn't give Titania any options when he took her. Why should I assume he would give me any, even if I did spare sending Venus to the moon?"

"Excommunicated?" muttered Apollo, unfazed by the threat. "That means there'll be a trial."

"Better get going," jeered Atomos.

"Let me go. I don't care what you do to me! I've been dead for a hundred years! I'm not afraid of you." She stomped her large foot on top of his own. Atomos didn't flinch. "I'm not afraid of anybody!" She sounded as if she really meant it, too. Not even the Leviathan had a shadow large enough to live in fear. Oddly enough, this realization reminded Atomos of the legend of the Umibozu. Venus struggled, trying to get loose. "Vengeance," she snarled.

"Quiet!" yelled Atomos. He gagged her mouth with his forearm. She bit down hard. Still, nothing broke his skin, not ever. "Now, tell me, Apollo, where has Agathon taken Titania?"

"To the courtyard, of course." Apollo shrugged. "Where else? This is not that big an island. What did he say to her, anyway?"

"He asked if she questioned the Leviathan or something. She said she did."

"That's interesting." Apollo nodded, placing his hands behind his back. "Well then, that's his choice to make. Agathon knows what to do with the Gyre. The Isle of Immortals is his. Still, in my view, if the Leviathan judges our piety, why shouldn't we be able to judge the Leviathan's will?" There was a long silence.

Then, a thought occurred to Atomos. "Have you changed your mind about the Leviathan being real?"

"Are you kidding? I'm a knight. Of course I think the Leviathan is real. I always have. It is real. You can see it. I just said that a minute ago, didn't I? I've seen it with my own eyes."

"You've seen its shadow."

"Yes," the knight admitted. "What's the difference?"

"How do you know it's real?" inquired Atomos.

"I have a secret for you, little Achilles. The truth is, clearly, whatever seems like it's most real probably is. Now, give me the ring. I assure you, no harm will come to you." Apollo extended his arm.

What could Atomos do? He was trapped. If he gave Apollo the ring, what would he do once he let go of Venus?

13

AN UNEXPECTED VISITOR

A small, squeaky voice shouted somewhere in the distance, "Apollo? Is that—is that you up there?" Atomos didn't recognize this voice at all. He scanned the scenery in every direction. There was nobody around as far as he could see, just mountaintops in the distance. He wondered if there'd ever been snow on them. The closest he'd ever seen was the frost on Trash Island. Perhaps someone was yelling from the bottom of the cliff. Who could've possibly been waiting down there this whole time?

"Can I get back to you later, Nereus?" yelled Apollo. "I'm doing something kind of important at the moment." He stared intently at Atomos, who held Venus still gagged in his arms. "Let her go, Atomos," Apollo added, whispering, "or we've got a problem. Do you understand? Do it. Do it now!"

Atomos felt as though he had no choice. He let go, releasing her from his choke hold.

"You're dead!" Venus was absolutely enraged, laughing maniacally. Her beautiful pink face had turned bright red. Her cheeks were glowing, thanks in part to the reflection of her armor, but mostly from the flashes of her toothy grin.

"Tell me, Atomos," said Apollo. At first, Venus was mad he'd cut her off, but as soon as he grabbed Atomos by the neck, she became quite satisfied with the silence. "Do you know why I ride this dragon?"

"Why?" groaned Atomos defiantly. Venus said nothing.

"I could've had any dragon I wanted, you know. Venus can testify." Apollo took the ring from Atomos. "I'm faster and stronger than Oberon, even smarter than Agathon himself."

"Well—" she began.

"Will you be quiet?" Apollo shouted, fuming. Again, Venus said nothing. "Listen, I could've ridden the black dragon if I'd wanted to. My dragon's the fastest. See how the light dances on her back?" He smirked, waving his fingers in front of his dragon's white scales. "Her name's Amaterasu. Isn't it just electrifying? Much prettier than her brother, Vulcan, though, unfortunately, they have the same red eyes. How many colors can you count? You're not blind are you?" Apollo leaned forward, inspecting Atomos. "Here, Achilles, this is what you will see: a kaleidoscope, a blaze in the corner of your—"

"Isn't Vulcan your dragon, Venus?" interrupted Atomos. "You're just going to stand here and let him say whatever he wants?"

"Won't you ever understand, Achilles?"

"You can't distract us from our goal."

"The knights are, truly, the best way to preserve the peace," insisted Venus. Atomos couldn't believe how far she'd fallen from the first time they'd met. She seemed completely sincere. At first, he'd thought she'd been rather nice.

"No, Venus. You know what? I suppose he's right." Apollo laughed. Venus seemed shocked. The bright white-and-blue dawn brightened their faces. "Everyone needs to stand up for themselves," he remarked, donning a sinister smirk. "Do you?"

Atomos had no time to react at all when Apollo shoved him off the cliff. He fell headfirst toward the ground. Atomos couldn't see a thing.

The back of his shoulders faced the cliffside. He had no idea where he'd land. Maybe, he hoped, he'd fall into a pool or a puddle. Instead, Atomos landed face-first onto the sandy, rocky surface of the beach. He was tired of hurting. The pain was so agonizing when he tried to stand. Falling and getting back up again and again was almost more work than climbing. As he pinched his eyes closed and tucked his chin into his chest, whimpering, Atomos felt the presence of water running only a few feet away from him in the sand. *So close*, he thought. Why'd he always have to fail at everything?

"Ex—excuse me. Hi. Hello, excuse me."

Atomos rolled over. He couldn't believe what he was seeing. The bald, misshapen knight, Nereus, was standing over him, smiling. Above, Apollo and Venus flew away on Amaterasu. How many of them were there? Everything was a haze. The objects around Atomos were spinning violently, but then each jerked back into place, over and over. Was everything timed to a ticking clock? Now, multiples of them were dancing, all at the same time. Atomos couldn't quite place what was really happening.

"H-hi, human, can I . . . can I be a part of your r-r-re-rebellion?"

"My what?" asked Atomos, rubbing his head.

"Your re-rebellion, I heard y-you and the guardians were s-s-starting one. The other knights are all g-g-gone now. I can help you," the knight said, rushing through every word. Atomos was instantly reminded of why he didn't like this guy. The sniveling idiot was insufferable.

"I hate to break it to you, mate. There's no rebellion." Atomos lifted his left arm toward the bald cretin. In his right, he held his throbbing head. "Here, c'mon. Help get me up. That's your first task."

"O-okay." Nereus did as Atomos asked. "N-now what?"

"Now, nothing." Everything was spinning. "Get lost!"

"But, but, but, s-s-sir, the r-r-r-rebellion?"

"There's no rebellion," yelled Atomos, holding his head. "At least, nothing I know about. The guardians all look out for themselves." He thought of Titania. Atomos rolled his eyes and bobbed his head side to side. Even though he could barely walk, he drifted back and forth like the waves; the irony of this situation wasn't lost on him. Still, Atomos didn't care. Irony and sarcasm weren't getting him anywhere. Clearly, he and the universe had different ideas, different wavelengths. Under his breath, Atomos muttered, "Now, if only— Where are those damn surfboards?"

"What?" questioned Nereus, catching Atomos before he tripped over himself. "What did you—"

"Surfboards!" yelled Atomos, whose legs were still very much in pain. He didn't care in the slightest if he'd interrupted Nereus or not. Every movement for him was excruciating. He didn't have time to be considerate. All the Atlantean needed to do was to calm down and breathe. Maybe then he might get a word out. *That might fix the stutter,* Atomos thought, *but what about the spitting?*

Atomos plopped down on the ground, not comprehending what was going on.

"Yes—yes. Of course, s-sir." Nereus went out to search for the boards while Atomos tried to hold down the throbbing in his head. He felt guilty. How could he know how it felt to have such impediments? Soon after, Nereus returned, saying, "S-sir, I-I couldn't, I-I can't—"

Instantly, Atomos forgot everything he had just considered. His temper was more than just lost. "Get out of here, freak! You don't think I know what you're doing? You're with them!" Atomos pointed to the top of the cliff where he'd just fallen from. Nobody was there. This time, the irony was lost.

"L-listen, e-everything can be t-talked out . . ."

"No! It can't. Get out of here!" Atomos threw a rock at Nereus, who yelped and limped away into the jungle.

Now, with that neurotic madman gone and not prodding him every five seconds, Atomos could finally focus. He followed what little remained of Titania's footprints to a pile of leaves. Now, he remembered. She hadn't wanted Apollo and Agathon to see them when they flew out of the cave. Lots of good that did them. Atomos took one board but left the other covered. Maybe Titania would be back. He doubted it.

Slowly, he got into the water and started paddling back toward the waterfall at the other end of the lake, near the library. The water was calm as Atomos glided over its surface. Still, he preferred salt water to fresh water. Its ability to produce larger-than-life animals was unmatched. From the whale to the giant squid, nothing compared to the connectedness of the Gyre. Atomos wondered if the Leviathan was even an animal, or if it was closer to a plant. Ripples formed out in each direction, fading behind Atomos into evanescence. The scene was so peaceful and serene. Was this how that frog in the river felt on the lily pad?

Atomos paddled off to the side of the towering waterfall. Mist enshrouded him from all sides. He stretched his arms out in each direction. Neither escaped the cloud of spray buzzing around his fingertips. How was he going to traverse this? Not with sight, that was clear, though nothing much else was.

Pulling himself up on smooth rocks and slippery tree vines, Atomos reached the top of the waterfall. To his surprise, he saw no library as he'd expected. The wall, the bridge, the tower, the gargoyles, everything. The whole structure was destroyed. If Atomos had thought it was a little rundown before, what was the rubble now? Unsalvageable. The cliff beside the waterfall was covered in broken stones. How many hands had slaved away at laying every single one of those? Had they been Atlantean or some other race? It shouldn't matter, Atomos thought, but it did, nonetheless. Trees jutted out of the ground everywhere. It appeared to Atomos as if Mother Nature herself had recaptured control over her dominion.

"All of this in a single day," he marveled. Was the mystical strength of the Gyre really that potent? Atomos still didn't understand how any of these plants had grown. What was a plant without photosynthesis? Where were they getting the carbon? Also, he wondered how the trees had known to grow in this spot. Even as he stared at them, it seemed they grew, inch by inch. Fortunately, Atomos couldn't ponder the implications of the monster trees for long. He saw the lone Atlantean canoe from earlier, tied to a boulder, floating in the stream, just as he'd left it.

"Hello? Apollodorus? Anybody?" yelled Atomos at the top of his lungs. He surveyed the ruins once more. Where could he be? Atomos considered that he'd ventured off to be with the other Atlanteans at the encampment, but why not take the boat? After untying the rope, as he was stepping into the canoe, Atomos heard an all too familiar voice behind him.

"H-hello, excuse me."

Are you kidding me? Again with this guy? Atomos turned around. In front of him stood Nereus, sniveling.

"Ex-cuse me, sir, b-but can I, can I join?"

"What?" shouted Atomos. "I told you to leave me alone ages ago!"

"Please, I w-won't be a-a bother, I-I p-p—I promise!" Nereus appeared as if he was about to burst into tears. "I just, I-I wanted t-to— I just—"

"How'd you even get here?" interjected Atomos rudely. "You couldn't have walked. Did you take the other surfboard? That was Titania's!" Immediately after saying this, however, Atomos realized just how terrible he was acting. The somber expression on the knight's face was more than enough to clue him in. God, this guy's feelings were so embarrassing.

"Get in." He shrugged.

"Are you s-serious?" asked Nereus, unsure.

"You weren't the one that destroyed this library, were you?"

"N-no. Does that m-mean—"

"Get in, Nereus. Quickly," snapped Atomos. "Now, before I change my mind!"

"Great! Th-thank you!" Nereus was overjoyed. It was almost desperate how appreciative he was. Still, he could do more than just sit there. After throwing the rope in the canoe, Atomos got in after Nereus. He took the paddle and pushed off the boulder. Nereus sat eagerly across from Atomos. "H-have you b-been here before?"

"To the library?" clarified Atomos, just as the ruins were pulling out of view. Why'd he want to know about the library? "Yeah, sure, I have. Why?"

"Oh, n-n-nothing, no reason. Just—just curious."

Atomos didn't believe Nereus for a second.

"D-did you- Did you f-find anything?"

"I did." Atomos shrugged. "However, I also suppose, in a way, it found me." Atomos decided there wasn't any harm in telling the sad knight what he knew about the mirror. For all he knew, Nereus himself could've been to the library a thousand times before. "I looked backward through a window in time. Have you ever seen such a thing?"

"Interesting," murmured Nereus, under his breath. "N-n-no, I ha—I haven't. B-but, as it t-t-t-turns out, I—I was r-right. Everything c-c-c-can be, be t-t-talked out." Nereus sat back with a satisfied grin.

"Nereus, I can push you out of this boat; remember that." Atomos smiled, but Nereus frowned, disheartened. "Okay, Nereus, okay! No need to play the victim," said Atomos, laughing. "I was only joking."

"Wouldn't be the f-first time." Nereus stared at his feet.

"You mean this has happened before? You've been thrown out of a canoe? That's absurd. Why? Did you try and talk your way out of that one, too?" Although Atomos laughed at his own joke, Nereus did not seem amused.

"J-j-just f-forget it."

Atomos recognized that this was a dark memory for Nereus. He didn't want to cause the poor creature any more undue harm. Also, in all honesty, he shouldn't be calling Nereus a creature, either, not even in his head. It didn't matter that Nereus wasn't human. Atomos didn't think of any of the other Atlanteans this way, although, admittedly, none of them were so unstable.

"Nereus, you're a knight!" burst Atomos enthusiastically. "You should be proud of yourself. Next to the guardians, you're in the most celebrated group in the Gyre!"

Atomos felt gratified for a moment, having tried to make Nereus feel better, but this was only a product of his inexperience. He wasn't actually being supportive, and thus, it was only natural that his encouragement went unnoticed. For Atomos, however, this was probably for the best. He began to think that maybe some companions were more reliable than Nereus. Although he didn't really know where anyone else was. How many people actually lived here on the island? Atomos chose not to think about the details. He was already lost enough.

"I'm, I'm th-the . . . I'm the messenger knight. I-I d-d-deliver m-messages. M-m-maybe I-I'm one of them, s-s-sometimes, but I-I doubt it."

Atomos nodded, paddling on. He considered a lot of what he'd just learned.

"I thought the consensus was that the Gyre didn't have class struggle?" Atomos thought back to his memory of all the tension on the mainland. Pueo had always helped contextualize for him. *No military, no police, no occupation, no taxes, no money, no life pressures, and only one semi-demanding religion. What's not to like?* Atomos chuckled to himself at the simplicity of the question. "In my world," he continued, "most people are divided. You're either born rich or you're born poor; most are poor. Nothing's ever done to change that. Tyranny is always the end result." Atomos couldn't help but think of Titania.

"Y-you kn-know, I-I like you. You-you're n-not as d-dumb as everyone says, n-n-no offense." Atomos wasn't sure how to take this compliment. "Even here," Nereus continued, "p-p-power is everything."

"How? What gives people power? Trade? I didn't see the guardians bringing anything back from the surface. How many weird fruits can this island produce?" joked Atomos.

"Trade? Well—Well, I'm not sure if I-I . . . Well, to, to pass the time, we trade in p-prayer; but—but that's about it."

"In the courtyard?"

"Y-yes."

"Nowhere else?"

"Y-yes." His beady black eyes widened. "I-I mean n-n-no!"

"Unbelievable," muttered Atomos, realizing the unfaltering loyalty these idiots gave to Agathon. This power of "will" was infinitely greater than anything Atomos could produce with brute strength. Again, he felt as if he were trapped inside a rushing torrent, unable to change his fate in any way. Perhaps it was the concussion, but for some odd reason, everything seemed like it was happening in doubles. "Well, Nereus? What are you going to do? You don't want to be just the 'messenger knight' forever, do you?"

"I-I p-p-p-pray."

"What?" Atomos himself had never prayed, not once in his life.

"H-hopefully, a-after the—the r-rebellion, the L-leviathan will s-s-still want to h-hear my p-prayers." Atomos thought it better not to ridicule the lunatic or mention the most obvious paradox in his belief system. Why refute someone's faith? Evangelization? He had no interest in asking anyone to subject themselves to any form of slavery.

"Why do you want a rebellion?" asked Atomos.

"I w-want to, to t-travel to y-your w-world and to, to s-spread our— our—"

"I can't believe this!" Atomos pulled in his paddle and set in on his lap. Regardless, they floated downstream. "You're talking about world domination."

"P-perhaps there may be c-c-cultural decline, but, but—"

"Human culture!" exploded Atomos.

"Usually, it's mo—most, most beneficial to the lowest c-class."

"You're talking about enslaving the entire human race!"

"No! N-no! L-listen! M-modernization is key. How, how many p-people are d-dying up there?" Nereus pointed his finger up, toward the sky.

"A lot," replied Atomos, regretful. He kept paddling along.

"Do-do you want that?" asked Nereus, more serious than usual.

"Individuals should always come before the betterment of the state." As Atomos was saying this, the messenger followed an invisible line with his pointer finger, tracing from the top of the Gyre toward the hills downstream. "*The vortex*," whispered Nereus slowly, in perfect, unbroken speech. He was right, of course. The courtyard was within sight.

"Well, you know what?" Atomos stood up. "I think this is my stop." In a single stride, he hopped out of the canoe and onto the bank.

"B-b-but, y-you, y—" The stuttering was back and worse than ever.

"Keep the canoe. I'll meet back up with you at the dragon encampment. Aloha." Atomos waved goodbye.

The Atlantean disappeared around the trees, dumbfounded. Finally, Atomos was rid of the maniac—although he was pretty sure he could still hear the imbecile fumbling his words, even after he was far out of sight. Atomos sighed. Why did he have such an ego again? Everyone was almost completely the same, with minuscule differences. However, even if there were no single alien force to take over the nations of the world, contact with this kind of technology alone would surely allow one of the countries to attack all the others. For the state to actually be ruled by the people, the way democracy intended, the people must have liberty and freedom in equal measure, but also, they must live their lives in equal part, in accordance with their community, alongside their neighbors.

Actually, never mind. Atomos reconsidered. No neighbors—at least, the fewer the better. The world would be a better place—more democratic at least—with more space between neighbors. Nowadays, there were just too many options, too many places to go, too many people to meet. All sense of personal relativism, moral and geographic, was destroyed. Once one cannot feel for the earth, believing that they are just as connected to the other side of the world, one cannot truly feel for someone else. It is impossible. One feels for that which is around them. All else is a lie.

The stairs leading up to the courtyard were as large and overbearing as ever. Atomos had half expected them to have fallen into disrepair like the library. He walked up slowly, swinging his shoulders back and forth. Atomos had some questions for Agathon, and he wanted them answered. For instance, question one: why had he been lied to? When Agathon presented him with the ring, he'd made it seem as if Atomos would be able to return home. Question two: why make up the lie about the spring water? He didn't care what religion anyone was. Last, question three: why was he being asked about a rebellion? Who else besides Agathon would've told Nereus to say that?

14

SONG OF THE CYCLOPS

Atomos was surprised to find that the courtyard was completely empty. He'd expected to find at least one Atlantean. Somewhat surprisingly, all six arches surrounding the fountain were standing still, as they had been, but its spout had stopped spewing. Beside the towering pools, Agathon's cup stood upright on the cobblestone ground. Seeing that it was left empty, Atomos picked the cup up and took it to the fountain. Even though the stream had run dry, water still rested in the lowermost bowl. Atomos eyed himself in the pool's shallow reflection. Nature had judged him most definitely. She wasn't going to leave in peace. No longer could Atomos simply say *out of sight, out of mind.* He couldn't forget where he was. He'd put himself into this situation. This was his fate for tempting Mother Earth. For all eternity, he was to be trapped in her otherworldly, submarine dystopia. Where was this so-called Father Sky? Did he drown? How long ago? If not, why did he abandon the Atlanteans? Did he move on, alone? Was this supposed to be simple solitude or purgatory?

Looking past the fountain, beyond the other side of the courtyard, in a grassy field, Atomos saw the giant, wandering cyclops, Argus. He might know where Apollodorus was! Atomos ran down the steps, careful not to trip over a protruding stone and fall like the first time they'd met in the courtyard.

"Argus," yelled Atomos. The cyclops kept barreling onward, not reacting to Atomos in the slightest. Atomos ran directly to the one-eyed, big-eared elephant man. As he chased Argus, who wandered aimlessly in the long grass, Atomos realized he'd forgotten just how large the cyclops was. On each side of the pathway, the tall grass towered over Atomos, but the giant towered over them both. "Argus," panted Atomos. "Won't you stop?"

"Keep on moving," he suggested, taking a short break from his humming.

"Have you seen—" asked Atomos.

"Next question, nimrod," returned the elephant man swiftly. He kept walking. "Don't ask me what I've seen. I've seen it all."

"Wait! Well, can I ask where you've been all this time?" inquired Atomos.

"I went out into the forest." Argus never stopped for a moment as he talked. "A fire was burning in my head." Atomos followed closely behind in mowed grass, intrigued. "I cut and peeled a broken wand," he grumbled. "I stared at a stream. After a few minutes, I saw a little silver trout. Then, over my shoulder, I heard something rustling on the floor. Someone called me by my name, a glimmering figure. She laughed and ran—"

"Argus," interrupted Atomos, "do you know where to find Apollodorus? I need to talk with him before the games."

"Nimrod," said Argus, peeking over his mighty shoulder. Who was odd? "Take your hands and brush them along the dappled grass. You feel that?"

"I think so." Atomos did as he was asked, although he didn't understand why he was being insulted. What had he done that was so offensive?

"Until time is young again, you'll search for your destiny, human.

You all will. This never changes. However, next time, lad, think before you think."

Atomos wondered whether this had been the problem when he went spearfishing.

"I'm not looking for my destiny, Argus. I'm looking for Apollodorus. Now, if you won't help me—"

"You'll find him plucking apples under the silver moon and golden sun."

"What does that mean?"

"I've no patience for those who rush their destiny. Now, leave me be."

"But, Argus, there are no apples in all the Gyre," objected Atomos. "There's no sun! No moon! You know what? There aren't even fish!"

"Then, I trust you haven't looked hard enough, Son of Adam. They're here. Truly, take in the beauty of the moment, young human. Smell the flowers, listen to nature; you will see. Someday, you will discover the truth, I know."

Atomos was dumbfounded. Nonsense! What was this, some allegory or terrible metaphor?

"I don't know about golden apples," said Atomos, unsure. "Do you mean like golden rings? The golden rings that transport you to the surface, the rings that take you back to the golden yellow sun?" He paused. "But why the silver trout? Why both the sun and the moon? Why apples?"

"Low-hanging fruit." The cyclops shrugged. Suddenly, he pointed to the top of the tall hill in front of them. It was the volcano where Atomos had fallen. "Come away with me, o' human child!" Argus gestured for Atomos to follow him. Atomos did. "Life happens wherever you make it; however, you make it matter most. Whatever you want to know, only your past lives have understood."

Did he mean his own past life on the surface? Atomos thought of reading *Frankenstein*, 1816, and the year without summer. Did he mean Pueo or his real father? Nature or nurture? Who was his creator?

"I can see that your path, however, is blocked by an illusion."

"Illusion?" Atomos was even more unsure than before.

"In the Gyre," the elephant man continued, "the greatest illusion of all is, in fact, our separation from the surface world. We are all a part of the same ecosystem, connected by the oceans. Our planet, our Earth, it's one and the same."

Atomos thought back to his many discussions with Pueo about the island they lived on. *Everyone is like an island*—that's what the old fisherman used to say, and *We're all one big archipelago.* Boundaries were natural. The space between spaces were critical to understanding overlapping ideas. Pueo taught that seclusion allowed time for reflection. Seemingly endless lengths of time were thought to be good for meditation; the same had been true for prayer. To hear that Argus believed prayer inside the Isle of Immortals had the opposite effect, however, was shocking. Everyone really did have an endless amount of time here. Atomos reconsidered. Not everyone lived forever. There was King Triton and the other players tossed into the abyss, sacrificed for the paradoxical Leviathan. Was it there? Was it not there? Was it alive or dead? Atomos had no idea. The answer was beyond him. It was subatomic.

If anything was certain, Atomos was certain he was principally uncertain. First of all, how was it possible for anything to live out there when he himself couldn't push past the Gyre's outer rim? Could King Triton have simply made the other player disappear with a golden ring? Maybe it was an accident and the other player drowned? There were so many ways to die in the Gyre. Although, presently, the only life-threatening situation Atomos could think of on the Isle of Immortals was the volcano. Most likely, that was because, at this moment, he stood right at its base, gazing up at its enormity.

"If I were to have fallen in," gulped Atomos, "not even the fountain would've healed my wounds, would it?"

The pair of them summited the volcano. Then, quickly, the elephant man turned his head and continued around the edge, humming his song.

"Fear, guilt, shame, and grief," responded Argus, at last, admiring the radiating heat from the volcano. "Do these words mean anything to you?"

Was Atomos afraid? No, not really. Was he guilty? Sure. No contest.

He'd caused a lot of suffering since he'd entered the Gyre. There'd been some very real consequences for what he'd done. Atomos thought of Titania. Was he ashamed? No, not really. She'd made her own choices. Well, maybe he was guilty and ashamed he'd left Pueo behind so quickly. Did he grieve? Most definitely, yes. He sobbed. His eyes dropped to his feet.

"You must forgive yourself, Atomos. Don't allow yourself to be trapped." The elephant man then pulled a stick out of his robe. Immediately, Atomos thought of the wand in his story. Argus pushed its end into the rocky edge of the volcano, twisting and turning it. "Once you clear your mind, forgive yourself, and accept your situation, then you'll find a new life and new love along the way." Atomos was more curious about what Argus was doing than what he was saying. "Once your attachments are out in the open, Atomos, energy itself will flow through you freely."

"That's all I ever wanted," said Atomos semi-sarcastically. "Energy." Nobody was more blissfully unaware than Atomos. "Argus?"

"Yes, son?"

"What are you doing there with that stick?"

"Fiddling," replied Argus, nonchalant.

"Why?"

"No reason." The cyclops was quiet again, concentrating on his wand. Atomos thought back to his time with Pueo. Perhaps it was the size that reminded him. Maybe the lengthy, misplaced advice was familiar, too. Ultimately, however, the comparison saddened Atomos. He missed Pueo. Their time together had been too short. Atomos wondered if, eventually, he'd think the same of Argus. He glanced over at the giant cyclops with huge, rounded cheeks and pointed ears. There was no comparison. The connection just wasn't the same. Even Argus, this great giant, was too similar to the other Atlanteans. Perhaps it was the robe.

"Argus? Where'd you get your robe? Not, like, 'you,' specifically." He didn't want to offend the gentle giant with what might be misconstrued as an insult. "Where did you Atlanteans get your robes from? Is there some sort of textile factory in the Gyre?"

Suddenly, a crack in the side of the volcano splintered. Argus didn't have time to answer. His stick caught on fire. Argus threw it in. Lava overflowed from the crack and spilled down the mountainside. The flowers in its way were the first to go; then, the grass; next, the trees. Before long, the jungle was engulfed in flames. Rolling across the grassy hills and climbing the trees up to the courtyard, the fire spread to every corner of the island. The blaze entangled Atomos, consuming everything. Once again, in the chaos, Argus began to hum.

15

THE CALL OF KTHULU

Flames filled all the valleys under the Gyre, propelling smoke in and around the little hills and small courtyards. The blaze surrounded the lake and climbed up the mountains. Trees fell in the distance. *Snap! Crack!* Then, from the outburst, Atomos noticed a bellowing noise echoing throughout the Isle of Immortals. The horn was blaring the melody Argus had been humming earlier, only much louder. There it was again. Atomos had never heard such an odd sound before. Then, immediately after, a gang of dragons roared in the distance.

Rawwwr!

"Can you hear that?" asked Argus.

To hear it from the volcano, Atomos thought, *there must be fifty or more.*

"That's the call of Kthulu." The giant beamed happily. He went on humming.

"What does that mean?"

"The games are about to begin." Atomos felt his gut turn over. He was also, predictably, quite light-headed. He couldn't even hold on to Azure last time. Maybe he should just quit.

Atomos and Argus started down the flaming hillside. Never had Atomos wished so much that he'd brought those flip-flops from back home on the island. Still, his skin was impenetrable, aside from that little hook he hadn't told anyone about. Atomos would be fine with a little flame, here or there. Toxic smoke was what bothered him most. His heels and arches felt incredibly hot. Luckily, however, he wasn't Achilles.

"You wouldn't happen to have any special chakras that could make me fly, would you?" Atomos knew his phrasing could, quite probably, be offensive to Argus. Still, he had to ask. Atomos had no time to be reserved. All suspension of disbelief was gone. His ambivalence was lost, forgotten. His mind was clouded. Judgments must be made, for everyone's sake. Time was inevitable, not inexhaustible. He thought it better to not waste anyone else's but his own.

"What happened to those Kthulu scrolls of yours?" countered Argus, staring intently at Atomos with his striking, single black eye. Atomos was shocked. How did he know about the scrolls Atomos had taken? How was that even possible? Was it too far-fetched to think the Leviathan and Argus might have the same sort of telekinetic connection?

That was it, the biggest problem with life, just as it had been back home: a lack of privacy. Solitude, isolation, alone time—these were all valuable, perhaps even more than communion. To Pueo, a lack of public privacy in the modern world had led to the collapse of personal attachment. Perhaps that's why everyone left him. Atomos thought back. Where were the scrolls? He was carrying them through the jungle when he ran into Titania. He remembered picking them up then. Could they be in the cave? No. How could he have climbed the cliff with the scrolls in his hands? He had no satchel. He must have left them buried underneath the leaves with Titania's surfboard. *Damn!* Atomos was infuriated with himself. Why hadn't he at least double-checked? Everything depended on Argus.

"I— They—they're on the other side of the island." He was so broken up he couldn't even talk. Every word was a struggle. His thoughts were thicker and harder to see through than the smoke billowing from the treetops. Was this how Nereus felt all the time? He pulled himself together. "Argus?"

"Yes, Atomos?" answered the knight, who stopped, mesmerized by the blaze. "I suppose you're lucky they're not here."

"Do you have any wisdom, anything at all, that might help me before the start of those games?"

Argus turned to face Atomos. "One of the Telchine kings was said to have reached this distant island, now called Japan, after having completed his royal statue. Since then, we've always shared a common ancestry. As you likely know, samurai were recognized and revered by the people of the island, like a great tsunami. Their lives, they recognized, were fleeting."

"Has there ever been a samurai in the Gyre?" asked Atomos, unbelievably enthused that he had been at least somewhat right about the style of their armor. Even the red suit seemed familiar. He pictured himself donning the piece.

"The last human to come to the Gyre came hundreds of years before then." Atomos sighed, remembering only now that samurai were relatively modern to the rest of the ancient world. He already knew that the last human was from ancient Rome. What a stupid question. He might as well have asked about the Aztecs. "Once, however," continued Argus, "I remember, the knights learned of a samurai who'd outlived anyone and everyone he'd ever loved."

"What'd they do?"

"What do you think? They sent the guardians."

"How long did the samurai survive? Is there another fountain?" Instead of answering, Argus pulled something out of his robe. This time, it wasn't a wand or a scroll; it was a pink pineapple—or, at least, it looked like a pineapple, only covered in a lot more fuzz and a lot smaller.

"What's that?" exclaimed Atomos.

"The fruit of a dragon palm. This is the only species to grow on the Isle of Immortals, besides these flowers." Argus handed the fruit over to Atomos.

"Why?" Ashes fell onto the seed as Atomos held it up to the light.

"I picked it up on the way up here. You don't want it? Give it back." Tiny white flakes fell all around them as Argus held out his enormous hand.

"No," said Atomos.

"There's your wisdom." The cyclops shrugged and turned away from Atomos. Once again, he faced the summit.

"In what world would I want to put a seed in ashes?"

"You tell me," giggled Argus. He wiped the corner of his big, black eye. Suddenly, Atomos heard a roar and felt a gush of wind pushing the flames away. This wasn't a thunderstorm; this was a challenge. *Swoosh!*

Barely missing Atomos, whose hair blew over his eyes, the rainbow dragon, with Apollo on its back, flew swiftly over the volcano. In his hands, the knight held a large, spiraling, white horn from which he'd likely bellowed the familiar but odd Atlantean tune Argus had hummed: the call of Kthulu. After pulling the spiky sea snail from his lips and circling over them twice, Apollo stared at Atomos in disdain.

"Hey, kid, don't you two have somewhere to be?" yelled the knight angrily, from across the sky.

"No!" yelled Atomos. The dragon's red eyes glowed like lava.

"You humans disgust me. Your dismemberment of sacrifice and rituals is sickening to me. Didn't you hear the call?" Apollo tucked the conch into his tunic. "The forty-second Kthulu is about to begin."

"What's next, the forty-third?" asked the cyclops semi-sarcastically.

"Are you stupid?" replied the archer.

"We'll get there when we're there," assured Argus.

"What about the fire?" questioned Atomos.

"What fire?" countered Argus.

Swinging his bejeweled bow to his back beside his golden fleece arrow pouch, Apollo promptly pulled out an Atlantean trident off his saddle, identical to Oberon's.

"We'll deal with it later. Now, both of you, off to the dragon encampment."

A gust of wind smacked Atomos in the face as Apollo turned and flew away. Still, he was in awe. The shining opal dragon, Amaterasu, was far faster than any Atomos had seen, faster than even Osiris. As he was flying away, Atomos thought he saw the knight putting on a crimson helmet. It was the crescent moon. Clearly, Apollo was living half his life in the shadows. What role did he have to play in the destruction of the library? Atomos was careful to avoid stepping on flames or scorching-hot lava while walking through the blazing forest.

He then realized the giant elephant man wasn't trailing behind him. *What gives?* Where was he now? How hadn't Atomos noticed the sudden silence? Perhaps the crackling inferno had distracted him. *Snap!* A tree fell over behind him. He turned, walked back to the edge of the tree line, and saw Argus at the top of the volcano, leaning over to pick up another flower.

"Argus? Aren't you coming?" He was a knight. Of course he'd be at the games. Instead of answering, however, the cyclops merely smiled and waved. Then, Argus turned and disappeared around the corner. Atomos didn't have time for this.

The heat was unbearable. He ran down the blazing hillside. *Crack! Pop!* Nature wasn't testing him anymore. Having arrived at the dragon encampment, Atomos saw the tall, square building floating in the center of the lake. Its large blue walls were attached to the shore by a thin wooden dock, at the base of which stood three large stone spheres, each of different sizes. Luckily, they weren't flammable, and the dock was too far from the inferno to ignite. As he walked across the panels, Atomos thought back to the dock on his own island. He had been so sentimental and weak-minded. Rebuilding a dock wasn't going to make Pueo come back. Reconnecting with Azure, however, might be more meaningful. He tossed the strange seed in the lake and walked up to the large, black, double-sided doors. After pulling on the golden handles, the door swung wide open.

The boy was bombarded with noise echoing around the camp. The fervent activity of all the island's inhabitants filled the room. He'd never seen most of them. Inside, Atomos saw the rectangular building was actually just a large tent hanging over a complex network of docks. The walls he'd imagined weren't actually real. The forty-foot-tall cover wasn't tall enough for the dragons, nor were the docks wide enough. Instead, the dragons entered from underwater. Walking past Atomos on both sides, there were riders everywhere: in the water, along the grid of docks, even the outermost dock which lined the perimeter of the tent. Atomos walked nervously through the sea of Atlanteans, bumping shoulders. He tried desperately not to fall off the dock or to touch any of the dragons waiting beside the dock in the water. One emerald, two yellows, each a different hue, reddish brown, burgundy, turquoise, pink, purple, and beige. Where was Azure?

"Human!" shouted a voice in the crowded dock. Instantly, Atomos recognized Zagreus's rough, scraggly voice. "It's good to see you. I thought you weren't going to show." Zagreus seemed to almost laugh at this thought, although, to Atomos, that'd been a real possibility. The fire ruined all his plans.

"It's good to see you, too," replied Atomos. "Do you know where I can find my dragon? You remember Azure, don't you?" Nothing, it seemed, had gone according to plan since he'd left the library.

"Yeah, sure. She's this way. I had her kept near the back with Zurvaan. I'm not sure why, after the stunt you pulled. Should've known you'd show up last minute, if at all." Zagreus led their way through the crowd, zipping around corners left and right.

"You said there was no point and to not even try—"

"You go on ahead, then, human. Obviously, you know what's best. It's not like anyone else on this island cares for their dragon as much as you do."

Atomos could sense the extreme sarcasm in his voice, slicing through the thick air.

"Can't wait to see you with that golden ring around your finger," laughed Zagreus. Turning on his heels, he walked away without even the slightest gesture toward saying goodbye.

Atomos scanned his surroundings, attempting to locate Azure. She was nowhere. Paranoid, Atomos started to run, passing dragon after dragon. He slid up and down the docks. Surely she had to be somewhere. Hopefully, she wasn't caught up somewhere outside, in the fire. Zagreus wouldn't have led him to this area for no reason. Suddenly, Atomos saw

Azure. Finally! They were reunited once more. Only, oddly enough, Azure wasn't by herself. Someone was riding her. As Atomos closed in on the scene, pushing past random Atlanteans preparing for battle, he saw not just anyone, but Nereus sitting on her back. "What do you think you're doing?" shouted Atomos. He waved his arms from the dock.

"I-I-I—" stuttered the bald messenger knight. Atomos didn't wait for Nereus to finish talking, but instead of just cutting him off like he usually did, Atomos jumped up onto Azure's side and then behind Nereus. Azure shifted back and forth in the water, adjusting to the added weight. Meanwhile, Atomos grabbed Nereus by the shoulders and threw him off his dragon into the water below. Atomos was quite satisfied with himself. He'd warned Nereus before that this might happen. How could the Atlantean be surprised?

Out of nowhere, Titania dove off the dock, into the water beside Azure. Atomos was shocked by this. He hadn't even seen her anywhere nearby. He wanted to ask what Agathon had done to her. Why hadn't she been banished? Had they made some sort of a deal? Titania lifted Nereus out of the water, onto the dock. Then, she, too, hopped up and stood beside the rest.

In front of everyone, with dripping-wet hair, she yelled, "Are you kidding me, Atomos? This is the way you treat us after all the help we've given you?" Everyone stared at Atomos, judging, as he sat on Azure's shoulders. Nereus shivered loudly, chattering his teeth. Atomos had no clue how to respond or what to say. "He was taking her to the front, for you!" He had never seen Titania so upset. "Nobody thought you'd make it in time for the last call. Thinking back on it, I don't know why I ever cared. C'mon, Nereus. Let's get out of here."

Both of them left, soaking wet, leaving a trail of water behind them. Atomos dropped his head into his chest. What was he thinking? Or rather, why wasn't he thinking? Why act without a plan? His ego had not only gotten him in trouble with Oberon, it had also ruined the only good relationship he had. Atomos hoped she wouldn't hold a grudge forever. What other consequences would this have in the long term, though? What was he going to do now?

16 THE BANISHED PRINCE

Hoot! Hoot! The last call echoed throughout the encampment. *Rawwwr!* The dragons were deafeningly loud in response. The docks were lowered as the last of the riders mounted their semi-aquatic companions. *Perhaps they are all connected through some sort of pulley system,* thought Atomos. Although he couldn't see clearly, he envisioned a vast network of strings hidden under the water, controlling the dock's movement. After everything he'd seen, nothing could've surprised him. A never-ending series of turtles and elephants could have carried the docks on their backs, and it wouldn't make the least bit of difference to him.

Nothing in the whole of his experience could prepare him for what was to come. Atomos knew this and dismembered his fear, piece by piece. Hypothetically, the unknown was nothing to be afraid of. He didn't have to worry about letting himself or anyone else down. What was he so scared of? Nothing. Still, Atomos felt his knees shaking.

Rawwwr! Suddenly, all the dragon riders headed for the exit, swimming in and among each other. Atomos had never seen such a turbulent sight. All these people moving at once—it was chaos!

What was it that Argus had told him? Picking apples under the sun and the moon—what could he have meant? Ahead, the emerald and burgundy dragons blocked him from advancing. Maybe Argus meant to look for the sun in the one and only place to see the sun from down here: in the mirror. No, what if Apollodorus was trapped in the mirror? Meanwhile, as Atomos was plotting, Azure was bumping side to side against the other dragons. The huge, black double doors swung open, and all the dragons took off, each swimming as fast as they could to find the gold ring. Some went left, some went right, some forward, and some backward. Atomos and Azure broke from the main group, who were heading for the edge to gain altitude. Some front-runners had already climbed hundreds of feet in the air as he watched. Apollo was in their midst.

Donning the red armor he'd taken after destroying the library, he stopped at the head of the pack, dozens of Atlanteans passed him by. Nobody had even questioned him wearing it. What was the point? The island was on fire. Cult worshipping was the least of anyone's concerns. Amaterasu reared back, pulling in its front legs upward, spinning 180 degrees in the rising water. Together, the two of them seemed to glisten like the dancing flames and water below: red, white, and blue.

Atomos held his arms tightly around Azure's scaly neck as they bounded toward the outer rim. Never before had he been so completely dependent on her, not even during the duel on the volcano. The sound of rushing water amplified as they approached the edge. The colors seemed more vibrant than ever. Still, Atomos preferred the darker, almost purplish glow of the shadows at night. As they ascended higher, over the Isle of Immortals, Atomos could see farther than ever before—that is, if it hadn't been for the black smoke. Even in the places where the fire hadn't spread, a reddish-yellow tinge filled the air. Gaps in the smoke were far and few between. Suddenly, Azure broke from the edge, sending a gust of wind toward Atomos like a ton of bricks. He clung on for dear life. Together, the two of them glided through the air, hundreds of feet above the water.

Atomos shut his eyes, crouched over, and bounced his feet against Azure's back, tapping nervously, trying his best not to fall. Just like with surfing, this helped maintain his balance—at least slightly. Still, he slipped and slid up, down, and all over the place. He wouldn't be able to keep this up for long.

Opening his eyes once more, Atomos saw Venus speeding toward him, flying on her albino dragon. No! Not Vulcan. He wasn't ready. How would he escape this time? She was only a few yards behind. Out of nowhere, Zagreus swooped down from above on Zurvaan, dragging her down to the trees with him. Once again, Zagreus had saved him at the last moment. In the distance, Atomos saw Titania grappling with someone atop Tyrian, but he was too far away to see who. The hot, red air made everything more difficult to see. Arriving at the library, Atomos smacked his head against one of Azure's spikes as they made impact. Then, immediately after, he dropped to the ground, landing flat on the rocky surface, headfirst.

Rolling over on the ground, opening his eyes in pain, Atomos saw a massive green frog perched on a chunk of mossy stone, staring him in the face. Although he was seeing double and the creature was a little more grown since the last time Atomos had seen it, the cat-sized frog was definitely Ponos, the librarian's experiment. The creature sat still, staring, with a silver trout in its mouth.

On his knees, preparing to catch the slimy frog, Atomos reached his arms out slowly. Ponos slurped down the fish. Then, after licking its lips, the oversized amphibian hopped away into the tall grass.

Croak! Croak!

A small tail protruded from between the frog's hind legs. *That wasn't there before*, thought Atomos. Was the frog undergoing some kind of reverse metamorphosis? *What's next? Is the devil going to grow feathers behind its eyes, or gills—or both?* Atomos ran to the collapsed stone tower where he'd last seen Apollodorus. The mirror room lay in shambles. Under a pile of stones, the mirror half trapped Apollodorus inside. His hands and forearms were all that remained. The rest of him was fully submerged, extending past the visible plane. Atomos grabbed the librarian by his arms and then caught hold of his scraggly, silver hair.

"What's going on here?" asked Atomos. "Bobbing for apples?"

"What?" questioned the librarian, still in a haze.

"Never mind," responded Atomos. "Look, I've got Ponos!" He held up the slippery beast. "He just ate a silver trout. Can you believe it? I didn't even know there were fish here on the island."

"Yeah, a few," replied Apollodorus, rubbing his eyes.

"This isn't a frog then, is it? It's a baby dragon." After Atomos helped Apollodorus back onto his feet, Apollodorus revealed the truth.

"True, Ponos is a hatchling, but he's unlike any other dragon on the island. He is one hundred percent unique. Did you know fungi are closer to animals than plants? Even so, the older trees still use fungi to help younger ones to grow."

"How?" asked Atomos.

"By transferring nutrients and immune resistance, fungi help trees absorb CO_2 more quickly and slow the process of decomposition. Like them, he has the ability to breathe carbon and convert it to oxygen, which essentially makes him almost a living, breathing toadstool."

"I don't understand? He's half mushroom?"

"No animal lives a comparable life on the surface—none, except for the axolotl."[6] Apollodorus scratched his head. *Do I really need to hear all this?* Atomos wondered. "What're you doing here, though, Atomos? I thought the Kthulu games had begun already. Don't you want to compete with the rest of them?"

"That's exactly why I've come to you, Apollodorus. I need your help to fly my dragon." The librarian looked petrified. "I know where Agathon hid the rings. The only problem is, even after I get the ring, I can't return home with it."

"Because of the curse, you mean? Because you'll turn to stone?" Apollodorus removed his glove and, on his finger, Atomos saw a small, shiny crimson ring. "The material I used to make this ring and to conduct my experiments is only found under the library."

---

6   Axolotl was the Aztec god of death and lightning who guarded the sun god and ushered souls to the afterworld. As the gods began sacrificing one another in a great war, Axolotl escaped death by turning himself into a salamander with the ability to regenerate entire structures like limbs, spinal cords, and up to even a third of their heart.

"You're telling me you haven't seen—"

"I saw what Apollo did from the tower. Unfortunately, I was preoccupied."

"You're welcome."

"Yeah, well, anyway, afterward he took my materials and spread my growth serum all over the floor. I doubt he knew what would happen. Still, I have this ring. During the Warring Period, they were used by the breeders. Unlike the other rings, the red ring maintains its power both in and outside the Gyre. I think it's likely, therefore, that if you wear this on your finger beforehand, a golden ring will allow you to return, unharmed, back to your world."

Atomos didn't have time to question Apollodorus further. Ash fell like snowflakes on their heads. He took the ring. They mounted Azure. Sitting much higher on her neck, Atomos saw how Apollodorus was much more confident with Azure, guiding her; in turn, she seemed more relaxed. Atomos was beginning to trust the librarian. They dove off the bridge and rode Azure back across the island.

When they neared the cave where Atomos had last seen the golden ring, Apollodorus turned back to Atomos. "This is all happening too fast. I can't keep doing this, Atomos. You go on without me."

"What?"

"I can't risk seeing Agathon. God only knows what he'll do to me if he sees me. I'll stay close by, though. What if I hide your dragon from Agathon for you? Then, he won't have anything to hold against you. What do you say?"

"I suppose you're right," murmured Atomos.

"I know," added the librarian pedantically.

"Azure's my first priority." Although, in truth, Atomos knew the librarian was just disguising his getaway. That'd be his plan, too, if the time came. Azure reared back, spreading her wings, and Atomos dropped onto the ledge below. He pointed to the trees where he'd hidden the surfboards and the scrolls. "There—you see those bushes? Now, go quickly, before anyone sees you."

Croak!

Atomos still held Ponos under his arm still. "But what about—"

The librarian looked back at his creation. "You keep him for now."

"No, wait. I can't take him in the cave," insisted Atomos. "He croaks every two minutes."

"All right, that's fine, too. Hand him to me." After that last exchange, the librarian was off, flying Azure over burning trees. *Well, damn.* He'd lost his dragon. Maybe this was his punishment for the way he'd treated Nereus. As her lovely, vibrant tail swung out of view, Atomos felt an instant sense of regret. What if they never saw each other again? She wasn't some prized possession to him or some extension of his identity. She was his most loyal companion. Atomos was wrong to let her go. He turned, walking into the cave. He hoped Titania was okay, too. The last time he'd been here, it'd been with her. She'd been so brave, confronting Agathon this morning. Would Atomos sound even half as intelligent? When had he ever known himself to do the right thing?

Titania told him that the Gyre needed change. This was his chance to change it, but was he the person for the job? Atomos sat and thought for a while. This wasn't a knight's garden, nor was it a guardian's, nor even the octopus's. This was nobody's garden. Echoes of the past eclipsed the future. He couldn't just grow anything here, not without light. The dragon palms were absolutely unique. But how did they spring from the darkness?

Atomos entered the cave. As he walked and walked, he saw and heard nothing but his own faint footsteps. Shouldn't he have seen the ring's golden light by now?

Suddenly, Atomos heard the low grumbling of an all too familiar voice.

"So, the great and mighty Achilles has come all this way to find the ring." Sinister as ever, Agathon removed his hand from under his robe, revealing the shining golden ring on his finger. Drawing his hand up to his chin, the light cast on his old, wrinkly face, creating long, eerie shadows. A faint glimmer bounced off his decorative armor. Atomos refused to answer. Still, he blocked the philosopher's exit. "Come closer. I can't quite see you, Achilles."

"That's not my name. My name's Atomos."

Agathon laughed maniacally. "I knew a man from ancient Greece who used that word once. Democritus was his name. We all thought he was such a fool—Socrates, Plato, and myself. Plato said he wanted all his work burned."

"Lies," whispered Atomos. "You haven't been alive that long. Democritus lived over two thousand years ago."

"Do you know what that fool would've done if he knew a redheaded child was named Atomos?"

The boy was unsure. Why would anyone care why his hair was orange?

"He would've laughed."

Atomos was surprised by this claim.

"The idiot would've considered it massively ironic, I'm sure. Democritus spent his life arguing that the gods never took human form, but his people, the Thracians, were a proto-Greek society and considered red hair and pale skin a sign of godliness. In other words, in his time, he would've hated you most of all. Imagine if he could've seen your face now." Once again, Agathon burst out into a violent fit of laughter. "Still, to think reality can simply be boiled down to indestructible atoms and empty space? The incompetence!"

"You didn't know Plato. You've been living in the Gyre your whole life."

"So, you've heard of Plato, have you?" questioned Agathon. "No doubt, then, you know about the allegory of the cave?" His black eyes gleamed in the golden light.

Atomos felt very uneasy. Had he fallen into a trap?

"Plato always knew there was more than one realm," continued Agathon. "He used the allegory of the cave to highlight the prisoner's dilemma, the story of a slave. When he first sees the light, his experience is beyond phenomenal, unreal even. His identity, however, remains hidden under the shadow."

"Humans know what's best for themselves. Don't force your ideas on me!"

"You saw your past in the mirror. What else did you see?"

He never told Agathon this. How did he know what Atomos saw? Had Nereus told him? When?

"The mirror shows us ourselves," revealed Agathon, realizing that Atomos wasn't going to answer. "Any other mirror would reflect your outer self, but how can you use this moment to impact your inner self? Can you see past your ego? Are you feeding the flames? I mean, in all honesty, how can you live with that scar?"

"What's it to you?" demanded Atomos.

"The mirror will often show us the past. However, sometimes, instead of remembering for us, it will dismember and will insist upon our future. Can you picture it? No, of course you can't. The mirror's plane of existence is unimaginable for us Atlanteans. Humans have no hope to understand, and by the look on your face, I'm right. You have no idea what I'm talking about. I bet you probably think this is all about plastic and the trash vortex."

"How'd you know what I saw?"

"You stupid child. You mean you don't remember? The guardians found you there. You think Venus and Titania don't tell me everything? Their trust belongs to me. Their loyalty is undying." Agathon laughed again. Atomos was getting annoyed. "Why don't you drop this act? Face it. You aren't mad at me. You're mad at the circumstances."

Atomos saw right through his manipulation. Still, with the golden ring in his hand, Agathon was too dangerous to get near. Atomos needed a plan.

"Trash! You are literal trash," mocked the Atlantean. "You really are the answer, Atomos; you're zero."

"Isn't zero the answer, though?"

"God, it's like talking to a wall," remarked Agathon, shaking his head. "There are many answers. One of them is light."

"Light?"

"Light does not bend or break when reflected off a mirror, but both,[7] just as I administer both harmony and balance to the Gyre."

Atomos smiled at the ridiculous claim.

"If you don't like that allegory, human, take the shine of a sword or a jewel; they work, too." Agathon held his ring up to his face. "They forge their power from the light, clearly, but only so much as from the darkness."

Atomos wondered how other senses fit into this theory. Yet, all that he could smell down here was the spray of sea air and the taste of salt water. There was no escaping it. This wasn't Plato's cave. But leaving that place, after years of living in darkness, surely you'd go blind.

"That's a pretty odd revelation," suggested Atomos, unsure how much longer he could keep Agathon talking. "A bit double-sided."

"Everyone thinks about how others think," said Agathon. "That's the ego. The question is, self-denial or self-acceptance? The mirror allows us to see and choose for ourselves."

"What else is there? Is another one of the answers death?" inquired Atomos once more. Agathon was growing impatient.

"No. Death is like love; it always gets even. Time and infinity each work, however, if those two subjects mean anything to you."

"Wouldn't infinity be like after we're all dead and forgotten?"

"Not mine. Yours, maybe. You're nothing."

"I don't know, nothing?" joked Atomos.

"Nothing," repeated Agathon, unamused, raising his eyebrow.

"Is there a negative infinity?" questioned Atomos. "Isn't that like saying negative zero?"

"Immaterial. You're trying to distract me."

"I wasn't. I— Why weren't you at the start of the games?"

"Apophis brought me here." Agathon started inching closer.

"Who's Apophis?" asked Atomos, backing up slowly.

"Perhaps you know him by his former name, Osiris. As you will see now, though, he's mine. He belongs to me."

---

7   In 1952, Schrödinger suggested that the different terms of a superposition are "not alternatives." Today, this has been reinterpreted as Everett's many-worlds theory.

"Where's Osiris now?"

"His name's Apophis."

"Like the asteroid?"

"Like the god. To answer your question, though, he's with Apollo."

"Apollo?" Atomos pretended not to know who this was.

"He's my most trustworthy—" Agathon scoffed at himself. "Never thought I'd catch those words coming out of my mouth. But, you know, who knows anymore? Anarchy has been capitalized upon. Innocence has been drowned. For what? Imaginary borders? A word called 'sovereignty' rules over every nation. Conviction is your slavery. Passion is your excuse. Your lie you all call 'democracy' will boil over on the surface the same way that old fool's lie about the atom did. Surely, somewhere, some rebellion, some revolution is at hand."

"There's no rebellion, Agathon. You made it up. You just wanted to get rid of Oberon because he's the heir of Poseidon. That's why you're so threatened, isn't it? That's why you had him expelled to the surface."

"I've heard all this—thousands of years ago, believe it or not. The first day Argus came to the Isle of Immortals, he was covered in sand, head to toe. I knew immediately he was a giant and a cyclops; that much was unmistakable, although he'd yet to grow the ears of an Atlantean. Still, even before ever drinking water, the gaze of his large, singular eye was already burning as black as the pitiless sun."

Atomos was confused. Did he mean white? Also, were all Atlanteans once human? "How would you know?" accused Atomos.

"Didn't you hear? I was a guardian back then. I've traveled long and far with your sun on my back, human. I've seen the shadows of vexed, hungry birds circling above me, stalking their prey in the ocean desert. Every night, the darkness drops, and yet every day, the light returns. Meanwhile, for our people in the depths, these last twenty centuries of sleep have been twisted into nightmares."

"They're your people! You're to blame for their suffering, Agathon. I mean, look what you've done!" Atomos tried his best not to give away that he'd been here, in this very same spot, when Titania had accused

Agathon. Why hadn't he just grabbed the ring last time? Atomos felt the cave wall behind him.

"You're right, of course."

This surprised Atomos. He didn't expect Agathon to be so honest.

"I asked Apollo and Venus to kill Zagreus," admitted Agathon proudly. "She was my beautiful bait."

Atomos was enraged. He almost reached out and grabbed the old man by his throat; however, he quickly remembered the curse. What if his new red ring didn't work? Atomos didn't like the idea of being turned to stone forever. Even if the crystal were to prevent that from happening, Agathon still held the power to teleport him anywhere. For Atomos to get back to the ruins of Atlantis, or anywhere near Polynesia, for that matter, he would need someone he trusted to wield the coveted gold ring.

Agathon spoke again. "You can't give what you don't have, and you can't teach what you don't know, little Achilles."

"Her own brother . . ." Atomos shuddered.

"Every ruler must remember, foremost, they don't rule forever," continued Agathon. "Besides me, of course." He laughed.

"Until Apollo inevitably overthrows you, that is," responded Atomos. He side-stepped Agathon who'd been, little by little, inching closer to the wall.

"Apollo would never betray me. Here, in the Gyre, he's important. He has an identity. Why throw all that away? Without me, the system shuts down. Without me, nobody has anything. Apollo's not even really his name. I mean, who'd seriously call their right-hand man Thrasymachus?[8] Certainly not me. It's embarrassing. Still, he's a very capable knight. He understands justice. That's what's most important."

"I don't mean to burst your bubble, Agathon, but just between us, the entire idea of the Leviathan is undemocratic."

"You question—"

"You said it yourself, Agathon. I've been blessed." *Finally*, thought Atomos, *the theologian will reveal the truth. What is the Leviathan? Is it*

---

8   Thrasymachus was a sophist best known for being a character in Plato's *Republic*.

real or fake?

"You are not like us, human. We are cast away by the skies, never again to see another star, nor moon, nor even the glory of the sun.[9] Still, in the darkness, we found a friend, and as opposed to the infinite, sole creator of the universe, the bystander to our destruction, the Leviathan has given us so much more."

"You really think the Leviathan is your friend?"

"Godfriend," corrected the philosopher.

"What does that even mean?" asked Atomos.

"Friend of us or of the creator? Friend of both? Who knows? Neither it nor I."

Was this true? The power of the Leviathan was really real? Was it a fish god or a wizard? Marlin or merlin?[10]

"Either way, in the end, does it matter? Friends are enemies. The destroyer is simply the creator inverted and vice versa. Cause and effect. I don't know what your theory of time is, human, but what 'is' can only be a product of what 'was' and the negative impact that will come. Whatever you may think, your future is bleak, human."

"You don't know what the Leviathan thinks!"

"Believe me. We're joined. The Leviathan's consciousness is my own."

"Why's the Leviathan so important? What's hope going to do for anyone?"

"Detached from our creator, we are forgotten, but under the shadow of the Leviathan, we retain our spirituality. Didn't you listen to what I said about Plato? The religion and community of Atlantis is, as a whole, at stake."

"A lot of humans might agree with you."

---

9   During their reign, the Roman empire replaced the Greek word for sun, Helios, with the Latin root word, Sol, so as to refer to the sun in the present day, such as with the phrase "solar system." Perhaps, to be Atlantean was to be without Sol. However, this connection is not bound to any one single language or people. The German word for sun is Sonne which, as a verb, can be transformed to Sinn, i.e. their word for sense. Thus, in English, sinning is not only a degradation of the soul but a misinterpretation of the senses.

10   One of the leaders of the Arthurian circle, a legendary sorcerer, "Son of the Devil."

"Whether you humans view your relationship to the creator as a myth or not has no bearing on us or to our faith. I'm well aware of the dying spirituality of your world. However, that is to be expected with your belief system. Ours is not so black and white. Light and darkness are never either-or, but always both. Nothing is all one thing or all the other. Nobody is. Not even zero can avoid the rule, as it, in truth, is always positive and negative. Can you see? The water hasn't muddled our faith; it's deepened our understanding."

"You've tricked the whole Gyre with your lies."

"What lies do you speak of? Democracy? What does it mean to you?"

"The rule is by the people."

"Thousands have been healed from drinking and bathing in the Gyre's spring water. The Isle of Immortals protects us, Atomos. Who are you to deny reality? Nature is the immortal ruler."

"There's a difference between attention and intention," noted Atomos.

"Prayer means different things to different people," responded the old man. "What I've found, though, my young human, is that sometimes just taking the time to ask the question can help bring you peace. Does comfort come from outside the body or from within? Does it matter? No. Nature is all that matters."

Atomos was hesitant to respond. He wasn't sure whether Agathon was confessing his devotion or impiety.

"There's no denying the spiritual energy of our semi-theology. Just as you cannot see a light's true colors without the contrast of shadow, so too can you not see theology for all its worth without the advent of atheology."

"Wait, so, what you're saying is, the Leviathan is a shadow of the world's spirit? I thought you said the whole Gyre was a spirit? Don't you get it, Agathon? It's a double paradox. How can you so readily accept self-defeat?"

"That's not what a paradox is. Do you even know the meaning of the word, human?" bellowed Agathon, enraged.

"I suppose not."

"The secret to long life and happiness are one and the same, little Achilles. Life occurs in the present; no past hour is worth more."

"But what about time?" How did that not matter? Was he responsible for all of it, then, past and future? Was this portion of the self something he was willing to accept, or was it the part of the ego he should deny? If positive was negative and negative was positive, the only way out was to have zero expectations. Still, that was only a strategy. He still needed a real plan. Father Time, the aging Aquarius, the long-winded Lord of the Sky—did he really control fate?

"Time is all we have. Remember it, distance over speed." Agathon smirked. He looked out the cave to the light of the Gyre. Atomos had discreetly been guiding them toward the entrance of the cave this whole time. "Nothing ever stops, so why would it matter if time ever went in reverse? I don't see any problem with it."

"You say things matter one second and don't the next, Agathon. Aren't you afraid? Aren't you terrified of dismissing the consciousness of your beloved enemy god?"

In front of all the knights and everyone who'd gathered below the ledge, Agathon lunged for Atomos. Like before, Atomos ducked out of the way. Unwittingly, the mad philosopher slipped hard and fell from the tall cliff. The fall appeared significantly more awkward this time than when Atomos had been pushed off the cliff by Apollo—or, rather, Atomos remembered, Thrasymachus.

Everyone stared. Atomos didn't know any of their names. Most still floated in the lake water, riding their dragons. Atomos safely slid down the cliffside, landing on his feet. Agathon didn't move. Nobody helped him up. Removing the ring from Agathon's finger, Atomos stood to see Apollodorus come out from the bushes.

"Hello, Atomos."

"Apollodorus? You were right, right about everything. The mirror, all of it. Agathon's true strength lies in his ability to make others feel happy—"

"I understand," interjected the librarian, one last time. He took the ring. "Now, you must go back there and start a new chapter, Atomos. You've got a whole world to save."

Atomos turned to see if he recognized any of the riders. He didn't. Apollo was nowhere to be seen in his decadent red armor, nor was Titania, nor any of the other guardians.

"Here, I want to keep good on my word." Apollodorus took Ponos from his pocket and reached out. Once Atomos took the slimy gift, the librarian rested his palm on Atomos, grabbing him by the shoulder. "Goodbye . . ." whispered the lost boy.

In an instant, Atomos and Ponos had vanished. This was no illusion. Atomos was gone.

The fishing boat was torn to pieces. A violent maelstrom had pulled its hull apart and wisped its metal casing into the air. The table where Pueo and Atomos had eaten dinner every evening was gone. Broken glass covered the floor, and huge swaths of dark, dingy water shifted back and forth. Suddenly, Nereus dropped in. His golden boots splashed through the brackish puddle. Nereus knelt, eyeing the trophies scattered around the floorboards while thick globs of rain began to shower down on him in the sunlight. A rainbow bowed over the bluish-green mountains in the distance. Nereus looked back at it.

"Orange," he said, pondering. "How interesting." The knight refocused his attention to the backside of the boat, torn away from the rest of the vessel in the storm. The pea-soup-colored tarp had been violently swept away with the rest of the wreckage. "O-Osiris!" screamed the stuttering knight. Instantaneously, the fearsome black dragon stuck its head inside the boat. Nereus climbed, using the creature's massive horns to pull himself up. "Come—c'mon, dragon, y-you're supposed to be good at this?"

The black dragon peeked back at him with its intoxicating eyes.

"T-take me to Oberon."

Osiris led Nereus from the wreckage on the shore directly into the monsoon at the center of the lake. As they plunged onward, Nereus was surprised to see the silhouette of a man standing on a small island, directly adjacent to the eye of the storm. He dismounted Osiris and stepped foot on the land. Nereus was surprised. Somehow, as if by magic, he had failed to see the ruins of a small medieval castle scattered around the island. Was he going mad? "O-Ob-Oberon? Is that y-you?"

"Yes, Nereus. Is that Osiris? Nereus? I can't believe it. You're the—"

"Agathon's d-d-dead," interrupted Nereus.

"Davy Jones himself. Dead! I can't believe it." The muscular Atlantean seemed far too calm amid the spiraling chaos that surrounded them. "Glad we made it out."

"T-t-t-thanks!" Nereus shivered violently, struggling to stay on his feet. Suddenly, the ex-knights saw the half-shredded fishing boat whizzing by the island, spinning around the edge of the vortex, and plummeting into the deep hole in the center of the black lake. Focusing his eyes on the scene, Nereus noticed eight gargantuan tentacles rising out of the whirlpool.

"I was talking to my dragon," joked Oberon, flashing a smirk.

"D-d-did . . . Did you—"

"Spit it out already, Nereus." Oberon mounted Osiris. He turned and faced the maelstrom. "What a beast! At last, it's our time to shine." Oberon and Osiris slowly inched forward, transfixed.

"W-where, where, O-Oberon? W-where are we?" Nereus didn't want to be left alone again without at least knowing where he was.

"This is Scotland!" shouted the dark prince as he twirled his new shark-tooth necklace in his fingers. Meanwhile, behind him, Osiris pulled a nearby white tree out by its roots and crushed it to splinters. The sky was very dark, almost black. The sun was eclipsed. "You've heard of lake Loch Ness, right? Over a thousand years ago, a dragon escaped through another one of the abandoned ruins of Atlantis, located at the bottom of this lake, here."

"The r-r-r-ruins of Atlantis are in a lake?" questioned Nereus.

"The ruins of the temple Noumenal."[11]

"N-nominal?"

"No, not nominal."

"N-n-n-numenoral?"

"Noumenal!"

"Neverland?"

"Never mind . . ."

---

11   In Kantian philosophy, this term means a thing in itself, distinct from a thing as it is knowable by the senses through "phenomenal" attributes, e.g. to understand the essence of an object, independent of any subject, to study the immeasurable, and to witness the infinite.

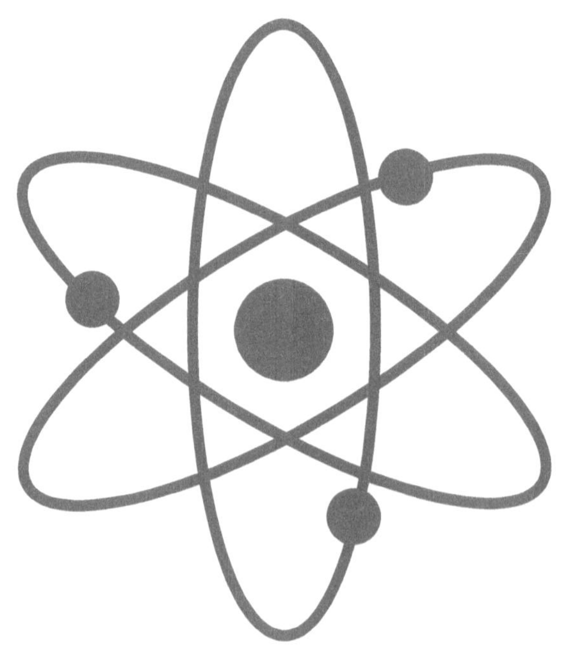